PELT
and other stories

CATHERINE McNAMARA

Indigo Dreams Publishing

First Edition: Pelt and other stories

First published in Great Britain in 2013 by:
Indigo Dreams Publishing Ltd
24 Forest Houses
Cookworthy Moor
Halwill
Beaworthy
EX21 5UU
www.indigodreams.co.uk

ISBN 978-1-909357-09-9

A CIP record for this book is available from the British Library.

Designed and typeset in Minion Pro by Indigo Dreams.

Front Cover design by Annie K. Hannigan.
Photography by Mark Ritchie.
The barbershop art is by an unknown West African artist.
Cover layout by Ronnie Goodyer – Indigo Dreams

Printed and bound in Great Britain by Imprint Academic, Exeter
Papers used by Indigo Dreams are recyclable products made from wood grown in sustainable forests following the guidance of the Forest Stewardship Council

Some of the stories have been published previously.

PELT published in Pretext (U.K.), reprinted by Ether Books
THE COPTIC BRIDE published in Heat (Australia), reprinted by
Ether Books
INFECTION published in Wasafiri (U.K.)
STROMBOLI, (as THE BRITTLE BEACH) published in Two
Plus Two, Staple First Editions (U.K.), reprinted by Ether Books
THE CLOCK TOWER published in The View From Here (U.K.)
NATHALIE published in The View From Here, reprinted by
Ether Books
GORGEOUS EYES published in Two Plus Two, Staple First
Editions, reprinted by Ether Books
CLAUDIA CARDINALE'S FLESH-COLOURED LIPS published
in The View From Here, reprinted by Ether Books
MONTGOMERY AKUOFO, FATHER OF TWINS published in
Short Fiction (U.K.)
AT THE MALGA published in Tears in the Fence (U.K.)
INNOCENT published in The View From Here, Ether Books
JANET AND THE ANGRY TREES published in Australian
Reader (ezine), reprinted by Ether Books
VERONIQUE IN THE DARK published in Tears in the Fence
TAXIDERMY published in A Tale of Three (London, Paris,
Berlin)

I would like to thank Ronnie Goodyer and Dawn Bauling of Indigo Dreams for giving short stories a go.

Thank you to my readers who have helped me overcome my shakiness: Emily Booth, Rachel Chu-McNamara, Omar Conzato, Anne Hallihan, Bozena Kristic, Andrew O'Byrne, Stuart Rosewarne, Sue Terry.

A special *merci* to Jenny Antoine for those tricky years.

Thank you to Ellah Allfrey and Robin Black for useful criticism and support at the right moments.

Thank you to Chika Unigwe and Rosa Rankin-Gee for their generous cover comments.

Thank you to Stephan Elliot, author of 'Priscilla, Queen of the Desert', for permission to use the lines in 'Taxidermy'. Thanks also to the producers of the musical and film.

Thanks to all my editors over the years for publishing my short stories. And to my family who continue to allow me to swim in words.

For Abraham, Grace, Emmanuel

CONTENTS

PELT
and other stories

PELT

Rolfe triggers it. In the way that is the way of all men. In his case a type of athletic bragging ruined by the self-defeat he hangs his hat on. I feel a plock and, with his surprised, involuntary retreat, my waters come splashing out, gay and heralding, whereby he bounds back to inspect the folds of his manhood.

My *obroni* baby will come this day. I roll onto my back and raise my knees in sweet excitement, the baby nestling back even though her head is plugged within my pelvis. Soon after Rolfe is agitating with a towel, peering cautiously at my dark opening. *No action there,* I laugh. He looks perplexed. Despite his thirty-nine years Rolfe is unfamiliar with the mulch of his own body. A fever sends him into studied ecstasy. The tumble worm in his butt, whose head and long wrinkled body I inch into the light, is repellent and edifying.

At the apex of his growth curve I suspect I must place myself. This is the man who continues to daub his hands on my sheeny back and breasts. He told me that in Ethiopia, his last posting, they call girls like me 'slaves' because of our broad noses and skin a shadow cannot cross.

This is Rolfe's first child. His wife Karina was barren. I have led Rolfe to believe that this is my first although I had two others before. They are at the village and I send them money. The midwife will no doubt perceive all of this.

Rolfe has been a maniac this past week. His wife Karina wrote him an email that she is coming here for a conference on small investors and banking. I have seen the flags up at the Conference Centre. It is going to be big. Rolfe and Karina have been working in different countries for eighteen months. There was a sort of split, Rolfe said, and they each decided to go their own way with work.

Karina is arriving this morning from Namibia via Johannesburg. Though Rolfe hasn't said it in so many words, I know this woman does not know of me, nor that I am full of Rolfe's baby. There is a certain satisfaction in that.

It is not an early flight so we stay in bed for some time as he has taken the morning off work. The girls have come in, rattling in the kitchen and complaining about their lives, as we make love in the slower, inflicting way he does in the morning. The last twinges as he rakes my buttocks are disturbing, so I pull away and his apologies are profuse.

Out of the shower he wears an uneasy grin and retrieves old cologne from the dresser. He traces a little elbow or heel that crosses the elastic of my belly then kisses me with guilt and pressure.

'It will be okay,' he says. And for some reason, '*I will never harm you.*'

Two hours later Karina arrives from Namibia. Blonde, tanned, petite. Small eyes placed at the extremes of her face. A fine bridge from the forehead to the nose where a slight bump hiccoughs the descent into cartilage. Thin downy lips and a wide jaw. Little breasts. Flat arse.

Rolfe brings her into the living room where I am sitting under a fan in an embroidered *boubou* and headscarf, naked underneath. Then there is a commotion in the yard with the driver and Rolfe is called outside. We two women are left alone.

Karina fights the first jolt. I am used to being treated as Rolfe's house-girl by visitors if Rolfe is not there to explain. I try to rise, but am impeded by my big belly and the lowness of the couch. Karina stands shocked at the end of a carved wooden chest. I climb upward. The woman takes a step back, treading on tall Rolfe's bare foot, her eyes fixed upon my bursting stomach.

She falls to Rolfe releasing mad ugly sobs.

Rolfe takes his wife to the guest room where the girls

12

have made up the bed and left the best towels. There is an *en suite* bathroom attached although the water pressure is not good. There are shelves. I think she should find some comfort.

When Rolfe went back to Germany last year I was just pregnant. He couldn't take me. I do not yet have a passport and visas are very difficult to obtain. He told me all about the trip. His town far in the north where his mother is postmistress and the owner of a hotel. How he skated on the frozen lake with his nephews and went on skis. Though I asked him to bring me photographs he brought none. He bought me a prickly set of underwear and a box of wooden blocks for our child.

Rolfe and his wife remain behind the guest room door for a long time. She is crying mostly. Long broken wrenching that comes from a subsided place within her. I hear Rolfe's tones, a murmur in their language, though these do not convince. This is such a Western thing, the dialogue and the praxis. I would have torn out his hair by now.

One of the girls – Comfort – asks me with a giggle what is to be prepared for lunch. Their assumption is that the real Madam has turned up, and I am just another hussy-made-good carrying a milky baby. No doubt this will be the speculation of the day.

When I met Rolfe he had just started out on the Obensah Housing Estate where crooked villas creep over hillock after hillock of red soil cleared outside the city. I was working in the office. He had a girl with him in a big jeep. A student type with straightened hair and good clothes. Later it turned out I was right. She was a student but she was back with her local boyfriend on the side. In the beginning Rolfe begged me not to do that, made me promise I wouldn't fuck behind his back. Before he even fucked me he made me do an AIDS test. Oh, he couldn't keep his hands off me and let me jack him off, but he wouldn't put his thing in until my results came back clear.

Sometime after midday Rolfe emerges from the guest

room and draws the door closed. The woman is no longer crying. They have been inside for one hour and fifty-three minutes. I am still sitting on the chocolate velour couch the same colour as I am, the couch where Rolfe – when the girls have gone – likes to make me lie naked. But I have been sitting out here watching the clock he brought back from Morocco, feeling our baby curl up in sleep.

Rolfe stands looking at me from the other side of the room. He appears very white. His eyes are glassy small discs. Other girls say the same thing about their *obroni* men: when their old wives turn up they become little boys.

He glides past me, plonks down and wraps his head with his considerable hands.

'*Was hab ich getan?*' he moans. '*Was hab ich getan?*'

You don't need to have studied German to understand that.

Karina comes to the lunch table in a black flowery dress that sucks in at the waist. It is long, below the knees, showing her swelling, resolved calves. She wears tiny rounded black shoes with no heel. Washed, her blonde hair now shows its icy cut.

She and Rolfe can find no way to address each other's faces, though she smiles briefly at Comfort lolling in the doorway. Her eyes look like she has suffered bee stings, or punches from a wild boyfriend, although I know Rolfe would never do that.

I touch Rolfe's naked foot under the table. He jerks it away.

It is uncalled for because I have made his favourite – *banku* and okra – hoping to calm his mood. His head snaps back in Comfort's direction.

'*Cutlery?*'

Comfort scurries off, skirt flaring in the hallway. Titter

from the pots. This is a meal which, in my company, he will eat with his hands, on occasions eating from my fingers. Comfort reappears with her boulder-white eyes over spoons and forks arranged like surgical instruments on a metal tray. Keen to see what will come next, she leans on the door frame once more, her bare toes twitching on the tiles.

'Go off from here, you silly girl,' I say in local language.

Her grin crackles.

Rolfe and his wife eat in silence. She pulls away a wedge of *banku* with the spoon, assessing its consistency and dribbling it with the sauce. She knows I am watching her. My baby moves a limb high up against my rib cage. She brings the *banku* to her mouth, glancing at me before she parcels it in warily. Her eyes water. She is forced to look to Rolfe, struggling. Comfort brings a jug of water and sloshes it into our glasses. Scant words are spoken in German. The woman perseveres with her meal while Rolfe's plate empties. I am playing with my food now, pushing a shallow indentation into the *banku* which pools with sauce, breaking apart the last shard of fish. Given the heartburn that will come later.

Rolfe pushes his chair back, going himself out to the kitchen for a beer. He gives a bottle to Karina and her eyes take this in with some relief. Rolfe throws his down while Karina drinks with jerky rapid slaking.

It is time to leave them alone.

I turn on the fan and lie down upon our bed. The food makes me sweat. I pull off my headscarf and my hair spills out. I wanted to have extensions done before the baby. Rolfe wants me to crop it short and tight around my skull – *sakura* – but he does not realise that schoolgirls wear their hair in that way. I am not a schoolgirl. I am uncomfortable. The food has started its burning passage up and down my oesophagus. Right now, I feel like sex.

But out in the living room they have started again. The woman, in a different register now, is talking more solidly with few breaks. Rolfe must have his head down, nursing his beer, the way he is mumbling.

'*Nein, nein,*' he says like a weak animal. '*Nein –* '

I put on the little Rex Omar cassette near my head and remember dancing to *Abiba-eh* in a tight dress.

I wake up at sundown. Mosquitoes. The baby tapping my inner spine. Rolfe gone. His wife.

Out in the kitchen Comfort is asleep against the wall. She knows better than to wake me when she wants to be dismissed. Cecelia has already taken off. I look into Comfort's open pink mouth and realise I will sack the pair of them as soon as I have the kid.

'*Where are they?*' I say.

Comfort's eyes open lucid and cocky.

'In the car, Madam. They have left in the car.'

The only time I have ever gone behind Rolfe's back is with Joseph who is a *Ga*. Years ago Joseph fell into a learning programme for street kids and met the coordinator, much older than him, from Canada. He has been to Canada twice and they are married. When he is in town he still sells stereos and cameras he has been passed. He knows the gangs that break into *obroni* houses. I think of Joseph and Miriam in their little house on the beach, the way he pats her on the head as if she has taught him to do it right. Joseph and I together, we are something. After Joseph, I cannot even walk.

But I don't want Joseph now. I sit in front of the television and watch *Sunset Beach*.

They come back in the stifling dark although Rolfe does not come to me. Because of the baby I shift in and out of sleep all night. They remain murmuring in the living room, opening more beers. At times, the woman releases a small, sad laugh.

Somehow, though there are no specifics, I sense the

movement of their bodies together. There is a change in volume, electricity. I sense their searching for reasons has fired off like broken flowers; that today's steeliness has finally eased.

With a shock, I hear them progress to the guest room.

I half-rise, cramping my upper belly and pushing the baby downward. She jerks, then begins to hiccough. I wait for each hiccough to *tap-tap-tap* inside of me. Down low where the head is already lodged above my pussy. Every tap is a drop of rainwater on my tongue setting off a shiver and recoil. I cannot hear them. They say that European women scream like cats and like to sit on a man. Well, this one does not.

Rolfe though he doesn't stay too long (there is pleading) accomplishes his feat. He comes into the darkness around me, washes lazily in our *en suite* bathroom and throws his whole exhausted length on the bed sheets where in moments he is asleep. He does not touch me or the wide berth housing his child. The woman by contrast is still awake, I hear. She is restless, charmed and defrauded by her man. Can't she see? She can. She is weeping in her room to the *lip-lip-lip* of the fan.

Later, I am pissing in the hall toilet where I can flush, with my thong at my knees.

Karina is standing there watching me, the dim light glowing on her nightdress. I pull up my red thong which she observes as it travels to the pouch below my massive belly. I always sleep naked. My full breasts swivel towards her. These are the breasts her husband sucks.

But she doesn't back off this time. Rather, she holds out her hands towards the baby's black halo.

'Can I?' she says, her eyes hurrying to my stomach.

She plants her hands there quickly. With her short square nails they look like sea creatures that you trawl up, webbed on my skin. But the baby is asleep and there is no movement.

She removes her hands and I know what it is that she can

17

feel. It is the whirr of my blood, the blood I have given to Rolfe's baby. She turns down the hall and I hear her close the door.

Back in my room Rolfe snuffles in his sleep, branching out for me. I fit to him. He swells and we sleep at length in this way.

In the morning Rolfe discovers that a thief has made off with the rear lights, spare tyre and both headlamps of his 4-door Mitsubishi Pajero. The driver, asleep in the boys' quarters, also protests that his bath towel (grey, if I remember, bone thin) and his *charley wate* are missing. Evidently, we were all lost to sleep. Rolfe sacks the driver on the spot and calls forth the garden boy, a towering northerner with a machete. The boy begins to whimper. Rolfe's Western discourse about trust and honesty falls upon keen ears however. The boy is listening for the word *police*.

Karina is watching from the terrace in her bathrobe, adding apoplectic asides in German to the guilty parties. Rolfe storms between the two men, this way and that, knowing that the unscrewed pieces were passed over the wall to eager hands on bare feet, and carried to a taxi at the end of the road. They will already be in various mammies' stalls in the spare parts market. I turn away. Rolfe looks so handsome in his draw-string trousers with his thing bouncing around. I'm sure Karina has noticed that.

Karina comes to breakfast in a mauve dress which follows her form but slinks away from it. It is synthetic and moves oddly, adding to the oddness of her proportions. She has a black ribbon tying her hair back and drinks juice, then harsh black coffee from a small drip filter she has brought with her. Rolfe is too angry to eat. He takes a short shower and goes outside to smoke. The woman's curiosity of late last night has withdrawn into a single grey tear that collects in her eye and wanders down beside the hillock of her nose. I hear her swallow in her throat. It is difficult to see the way that Rolfe would fuck

18

her: which games they would play in the rooms of the house. She stands up and collects a briefcase and a laptop. The taxi Rolfe has ordered is honking at the gate. He urges her out the frosted glass door.

The day sets out to be long and cantankerous. Rolfe telephones me from the office and tells me to call Joseph to find out what I can about the parts. I tell him I won't accuse Joseph of theft. Rolfe replies that Joseph will most certainly know where the parts went. His voice is growing exasperated thorns. While I know this is not the case, I lie: 'He's travelled,' I tell him. 'Last week.'

Rolfe's thorns break my skin. He says that is bullshit, that yesterday he saw Joseph on the beach. 'Oh?' I say, sweat welling. 'So you softened her up on the beach?'

Rolfe's line goes dead.

I call Joseph and he is around here in ten minutes, sitting on the other chocolate double couch. I send Comfort to do the shopping. Cecelia has not even turned up.

Naturally, Joseph wants to know if that was the old German wife Rolfe left behind. 'Well,' he says laughing, 'I didn't think she was his sister.' He calls her 'no-bum' and 'tuna legs' and 'fish-head-soup face' and seems to derive great satisfaction from this. I give him a beer and he presses behind me, so hard in the morning, but I move off, burning softly. Not today. Of course he knows who took the parts, but he won't get them back without a show of cash for his trouble. I try - my knees fall open - but Joseph will not be tinkered with in this respect. Soon after he gets up to leave, the beer bottle sitting in a lake miles away from its straw coaster. I hear his bike clanking along the road.

Comfort comes back, prepares *wackye* and serves it up for the three of us for lunch. I wait for a taxi to trundle up in the sand outside the gate but neither of them arrives. Comfort minces in at regular intervals to remind me that Master Rolfe and Madam Karina have not come home. By three o'clock, too incensed to yell, I throw the bottle of Malta Guinness I am drinking in her direction, which shatters somewhere behind her on the wall.

I drag my body off, tearing away my clothes, standing full and cantilevered in the shower. The water pressure is good. Water skitters off the chute of my upper belly, now emptier of my baby's limbs given these too have dropped into my pelvic cradle. My lower belly thrusts out to hold the heavy teardrop of liquid and flesh. My inside out belly button, the lobe of skin that Rolfe likes to lick, trembles black and divulged under the water.

It is too hot to lie on our bed. I wrap up my hair and choose a dress. Outside on the road I tap the roof of a taxi. A pair of pale heels is kicked out of the passenger window. The driver takes me downtown to the hotel that Rolfe and I frequent, where I have learnt to swim under his instruction. It is an inner city place where the *obroni* do not come. There are too many mosquitoes and the food gives you the runs. The pool has blue molten lights and we swim under the black blowsy palms at night.

I pay the driver and walk through the lobby to the garden outside. Certain air crews stopover here – the Ethiopians and the Egyptians – and I dislike the stares of these men over my body. Rolfe never wants me to come here alone for that very reason, also because I think he is worried I might drop like a stone to the bottom of the pool. With our baby.

It takes some courage but I remove my dress and walk over to the open shower, while two local Lebanese teenagers eye my ample form. It makes me feel sticky. There is nothing so exposing as having your body's naked act and its consequence protruding for all to see. Then, under the far palms, I see them. Rolfe and Karina. On two loungers pushed together on the grass. Inches apart with beer bottles collected on a small table.

Rolfe scratches his backside, then transfers his open hand to her flank, while hers cups one side of his face and he nuzzles it.

I step down out of the shower recess onto the cement surrounding the curved pool. Though the Lebanese boys have made rude comments, the two Europeans have not seen me, so avid is their talk. I look across to my handbag with its possibility of retreat. If I walk away, maybe this moment will never have occurred. But then I glance over to them and Karina catches my eye.

It is not hard to decide what to do next. I pace towards the wide tiled steps dissolving into the shallow end of the pool. I walk up for the grandest entrance possible, breathing in sharp each time the balls of my feet make contact with the grainy hot surface. I think of Joseph and Miriam in the beach house. How he pats her on the head. How he fucks me so well and then rides his bike off. How these people always try to make fools of us.

Rolfe rises. Karina pulls away. His face blurs. The waiter digs in his feet and attracts his colleague to the scene. The water trembles up my thighs, through my panties, up the bulwark of my belly. I begin the breast-stroke, frog kicking my legs as I have been taught, dipping my face into the water as my forearms clear a path.

Rolfe is standing. His balls and cock are squashed to one side from the way he was lying down. Though they soon fall into place. He opens his mouth to call my name, realises he has quite an audience, and instead rubs the back of his hand across his mouth. He reaches for his beer on the low table, Karina taking this chance to whisper her startled opinion. I am gliding now, past where their toes were almost intertwined before, and Rolfe can but follow me with the circling, desperate steps of a tall man on a hot strip of cement.

At the far end, in the embrace of a bending palm, he seethes at me, crouching.

'*This – this – you realise – this is foolish – you take*

yourself home. TAKE – YOURSELF – HOME – '

His eyes are locked on my face and yet do not centre upon my own eyes until the words have been spoken. Then they fill with sorrow and shock like a wound filling with blood. They darken.

'Just go home. I beg you. She will leave. She is nearly gone. I *beg* you,' he says as he bends closer.

But no extended hand or kiss of confirmation. He rises, adjusts the squished balls again and returns to the other couch with its pair of eyes.

Before leaving I order a tonic water, which I used to drink with gin before the baby. I ask Osman to put in some gin. Perhaps this is why it happens so afterwards.

I return to the house promptly, put on my indoor dress and turn on *Sunset Beach*. Comfort is heating palm oil for fried plantain. It smells as though, of her own initiative, she has prepared bean stew. Already I feel the heartburn and the long lonely night.

Rolfe and Karina clatter through the gate. This time the taxi has been soundless and I have not heard them bartering for their fare on the street. There is some talk in German on the steps as they carry up their bags. Over the television show, I can hear Karina bossing him.

I walk out into the kitchen to look for a Malta Guinness and there they are, Karina handing Rolfe a cold beer from the fridge. Comfort has just thrown the first disc of gingered plantain into the crackling oil, the way Rolfe likes it.

I move over to the pan, grab the heavy handle and manoeuvre it into the centre of the small room, its contents sloshing and spitting. It splatters a little onto the linoleum. Rolfe puts a protective arm across his wife, whose eyes leap towards him. Comfort lunges into the laundry. The pan is heavy and so far I am holding it with one arm only, although we can all see

22

that this is beginning to wilt. Oil slurps over, again, onto the floor. The plantain has in this short time become a crisp.

Rolfe's face staggers. I watch its transformation. His barren shock goes someplace else, gradually. It is pulled apart, the terror dissolving into little shards of reckoning, little mushroom clouds of capitulation. One by one his features recede: his eyebrows lengthen, smoothing the labour of his forehead, his nose loses its hitch, the muscles supporting his mouth begin to fail.

They are trapped, too, at this end of the kitchen. The woman opens her mouth to speak but Rolfe's eyes flare at her. He turns to me. It is apparent that my single arm outstretched beyond the arc of my belly could at any moment collapse. And yet Rolfe's features have attained the expression I desired.

He smiles at me. Recognition and hunger are plunged in deep strokes on his face. I have never seen a man hungrier.

Gently, he moves. With his help, the pan of oil is returned to the cooker.

That night Karina packs her bags without tears. Rolfe escorts her formally to the front gate. She moves into a hotel for the duration of the conference, the one closest to the airport.

THE COPTIC BRIDE

Last month my brother unexpectedly came back to Sydney with a fiancée from Ethiopia. Adam had woven a career through humanitarian agencies across the world, bought a house by the harbour and an apartment in New York, and had crossed the Sahara. He left us eighteen years ago and there was a week of undisputed turbulence whenever he came back.

I met them at the airport. The girl was not the fumy supermodel like David Bowie's wife. She was small, chesty and not very dark. I spotted Adam parcelling their documents away and steering the heavy bags. She followed in his tailwind.

'Adam!'

'Jim!'

We came together and I felt his resolve had softened – he was no longer working out. We separated and he introduced Laila who, though she had a jewel of a smile, had bad skin and a bulky, unattractive nose. My first thought: strange, given Adam has had a run of flawless women.

We drove out from the airport and Adam briefed me on the trip. They'd been back to headquarters, where he had to chase up some tenants subletting the apartment. They'd also had a rest and done some shopping, he said, *finally out of that place*. He glanced behind at Laila watching out the window. I looked up in the rear-view mirror and she smiled graciously back, her hair in loose springs against my tan upholstery.

We crossed the Anzac Bridge into the suburbs. Adam explained the Madonna's bra concept and I saw her cottoning on. In Ethiopia they'd had Bono campaigning for stick figure kids. Here we have a bridge wired up like Madonna's C-cups.

They were staying at Mum and Hadley's place in Drummoyne for a day or so before we all went to the lake. Mum's second exhibition had just opened in Woollahra so she and

Hadley weren't at home. I found a parking place and Adam and I pulled out their two suitcases onto the footpath. He breathed in deep, looking down to the sailing club where he had smoked so many joints, where he used to take Leanne Banks into the bush, where he'd even torn the rudder off a Flying Eleven on a broad reach. The bay was glassy, it had that untroubled hue. But in an hour the wind would be tossing it.

'You heading back to work then?' I had taken the morning off, but sensed that Adam needed some breathing space before Mum hurtled home.

'Yes, ought to rush. Catch you tonight?'

Adam opened Laila's door and his eyes fell upon her dozing. She had more hair on her cheek than a woman should have, on skin that was a tired yellow-green. Her eyebrows were ragged above her firmly closed eyes like Frida Kahlo asleep.

My mother adored Laila. Halfway through the afternoon she called to anoint me with her unqualified joy. I suspected it was hardly Laila she adored, but the prospect of a brown daughter-in-law and exotic grandchildren requiring the occasional visit to New York. Mother, on the overcrowded and whirring canvas of her life, sought such flares. She had married a plumber, given birth to Adam, lived with a sculptor and then had me. Now there was Hadley, a serious interior designer who pushed her photography and had taken her to New Mexico.

'Have you spoken with Laila?' I asked her. I had Ruben with me, in the St. Leonards office.

'We've just had coffee,' she said. 'I thought I'd better get back and prepare them some lunch. Adam's on the *divan* asleep.'

Working in the Eastern Suburbs and a stay in London last year had brought about an upgrading of Mum's vocabulary. It was sad to see *couch* turfed out.

'She's so adorable. I'm so happy for them. Are you coming over to dinner? When will you be following us up to the

26

lake?'

I replaced the phone and moved away from Ruben's eyes. In the aftermath, you wonder how you ever loved, as if it were some abject emotion that had to be slaked. Light from outside spooled over him as he released my apartment keys onto the desk. I watched his shoulders retract, the sweat peppery on my lip, my neck muscles beginning to unclench. In a year from now the pull will have left the pair of us.

The next day the traffic was hell out of Sydney. I organised food for the cats and read Ruben's final audacious message, picturing his broad fingers smudging the digits. I switched off the phone. The northern suburbs were pinioned out down to the last house on stilts between the trees. I opened my window at a pile-up just beyond the Hawkesbury. The scent of eucalyptus came through, perfume of the stolen land. The traffic filed through two sandstone walls quilted with dynamite triggers. In the car next to me I saw a pair of young urbanites in profile, metal piercings tucked into their fair skin. I thought of Ruben's blue-laced tattoo dissolved into his chest. How arcane it had been at the outset; how quickly it had begun to date.

Mum had rushed away from Sydney with shopping bags of delicatessen food, not to be diminished by a son who employed cooks and servants. Traditionally, she overreached for Adam, and this time the foreign fiancée compounded her will to impress. The fridges were stashed with local wine and Tasmanian cheese and tubs of pâté. Hadley hoisted up cartons of beers from the boat shed down on the water. That was where Mum had put the visitors, in the wood-planked room over the jetty sliding into the grey lake. I was in the spare bedroom in the main house. I unpacked my things into the little pinewood set of drawers, pulling on old porous clothes steeped in salt. In the bathroom out the back I had a quick wank and released the drama of the last few days.

Mum was in the kitchen pressing the base of a

cheesecake, her old faithful.

'Hadley's rigging up,' she said.

Sure enough, I saw the mast of Hadley's prized 20-footer down by the jetty. The mainsail went shimmying up.

'You're not going out, Ellen?'

Mum's eyes lifted at the untimely use of her Christian name. Now that Adam was here with us, it belonged to another intimacy.

'No, darling. See if the others are interested. Mind their beers are cold.'

But it seemed Hadley was heading out alone, as we all knew he preferred. I saw Adam push him off the jetty and turn around, walking with tender feet over the grain of the wood. I saw the looseness in his thighs and the curve to his belly. Even his arse looked rounder and shook like a woman's. He disappeared from my line of vision. I wandered down the lawn and made my way to the steps.

They were on lazy chairs in the sun, close to the water. Laila had gained some colour and appeal, lying in a white bikini with her hair unreeled around her. She lifted onto her elbows and her breasts rolled down comfortably, she opened to him. Adam sat up on the other chair, leaning over to spread his palm on her belly and they kissed hard, the first expression I had seen of my brother's conquest. Hadley, now beyond the shelter of the point, hit the mild nor'easter and tacked too early, sending the sails luffing. As always, he took an age to cleat the sheets.

After Mum's rich seafood and heavy-handed salads we sauntered down to the waterfront. Hadley set about lighting a fire with his stringy tanned legs and a packet of BBQ lights. Laila watched him stoke the flames as the dry gum leaves and twigs crackled. Hadley stood back as smoke lifted towards Mum manoeuvring down the steps with a tray of drinks.

'We have eucalyptus trees all around Addis,' Laila was

28

saying to Hadley in a light, thoughtful voice. He and I listened to her, neither of us able to tend the conversation.

Adam stepped in. 'They were introduced by the Dutch around sixty years ago to combat soil erosion.'

'Well, no,' said Laila. 'You're wrong, Adam. They were brought in from this country by our Emperor Menelik when he made Addis Ababa our capital, early last century. They were lacking in wood and he believed the species would be favourable in our climate. In fact, as you have seen, they have flourished.'

In terms of dinner party theatre, Adam had had years of training. In Nairobi I'd seen how polished he had become, his resilience. Yet here was his girlfriend with a PhD who worked in some outpost reminding him of history's wonky path, catching him out here in front of us. Adam sank down, grew into *sulky* Adam whom we all knew well and began to bite his thumbnail, a forty-year habit. Hadley stood up so fast you could see his eyes quiver. He staggered over to uncap another beer. Mum who was oblivious plonked the tray on the table and rubbed her eyes from the smoke.

'I heard the Banks arrive earlier,' she said. 'Adam, you remember Martin and Deidre? You used to sail with Dean.'

Poor Ellen hovered over her omission of Leanne, Adam's long-time girlfriend, Dean's little sister. When I saw Leanne last, she had three kids and was still whippet thin. She had just divorced. Laila, who knew about her Emperor Menelik but could not know about Leanne, walked over and prepared twin whiskies on ice. She handed one to Adam.

'No thanks,' he said uncaringly.

Laila paused in front of him.

'I'll take it,' I offered.

I heard them in the night. I'd left Hadley and Mum for some time alone in the house and was taking a solitary walk along the waterfront. I went to the end of every jetty that wasn't fenced off and stood listening to the stays clanking on the masts and the hulls rocking and the slapping water. I felt Ruben's absence along my skin and the times we had stolen here together from the city unfurled in my head. But Ruben and I had not given our intentions good government, and he hated the finicky rules of sailing and the slimy bed of the lake. Now the sounds muffled together in the dark, providing generous consolation. I gave Hadley and Ellen enough time to make love and drift to sleep, the curtains skating over their interlocked bodies, then headed back around the boat shed. Two doors down from us the lights were on at the Banks' house and I heard the kids were still up watching a noisy car chase on T.V. According to Deidre, a long-standing tennis companion of my mother's, Leanne's ex had gone interstate and she was seeing a Maori guy.

In the boat shed I heard Adam and Laila arguing. My brother issued a sentence and the girlfriend spliced it blade thin, until it wobbled and fell flat. From Adam's tone I could sense she had just about pushed him too far. When Adam's fuse frayed to the end you needed an almighty head start: as a kid I had climbed roofs and stayed bolted in the spare bathroom for hours to avoid his fists. I tried to picture them. Adam curled on the couch trying to shut her out, gritting his teeth for control as her high-pitched voice climbed in circles. The girlfriend in the unfamiliar boat shed with Mum's early black and white prints of the lake in pastel frames.

I heard the wicker chair thrown back and the table grate over the floorboards. Someone was taking a lunge. I heard a body fall unevenly and a quick scuffle on the wood. Against everything that I had considered proven within myself, I grew hard.

I woke up to the sounds of Mum and Laila taking off on a shopping expedition into town. My room in the old brick house had a hint of air passing through in the mornings but by mid-afternoon it reverberated with heat. Consequently it was not possible to sleep until late at night when the damp of the lake permeated the walls. I rolled over and retrieved a book. Occasionally I let my mind wander to Ruben in slumber, his paws suspended in endearing inactivity on the sheets. But I closed this away. I thought of his silver jeep reversing in the parking lot, how little and pretentious the car seemed, how its arrival had once unsteadied my gut.

Adam was in the kitchen wearing a loose shirt with a Coptic cross embroidered over his chest. As he opened the newspaper one of the long sleeves dipped into his mug of coffee.

'Bugger!'

He squeezed out the coffee and settled at the table.

'Comes with dressing exotic,' I said.

'Oh, hiya,' Adam replied, his pale eyes crystal clear this morning. I wondered about the girlfriend and the debris of furniture.

'Hadley?'

'He's out in the old boot. Praying he remembers where he sank the crab nets.'

'And you guys? What are you up to today?'

Adam mumbled into the newspaper. Born Sydneysider, he still suffered the real estate. 'I was thinking of taking Laila over the other side, over to the beach. Like to come?'

The tautness around his eyes saying, *Whatever you do, don't come.*

'No thanks. I think I'll stay here.'

I poured some coffee and shook out some supplements.

'You still on that stuff,' he said without lifting his head. Ten years back, before he started the good life and broadened, Adam's body had been sublime.

'Can't let down the team.'

Adam looked over. Decades ago, on a packed suburban bus, Adam had been wearing nearly the same expression when he shot the calf between the eyes. 'Which *team* is Jim on?' he'd cried, cracking up, joined by the entire bus. Every face had swung around to the blanched kid in shorts.

But now I was unfazed. I returned the usual hardy smirk. The year Adam crossed the Sahara a group of Scandinavians had been kidnapped by some Tuaregs and a man the same age as my brother escaped into the desert to his death. I used to play with the idea that it had been Adam lost in the dunes, crying like a baby, nursing his last thoughts. Whenever Adam came back the image was never far off in my head. That way, my gratefulness that it hadn't been him: Adam never realised he had to earn it. I opened the television section of the newspaper. I saw *The Guns of Navarone* was on in the blind spot from two till four. I pictured Mum and Hadley downing *pinot grigio* on the water, and Adam and Laila tiffing at the beach.

'When did you guys decide to get married?' I asked.

Adam closed the newspaper and took me in.

'It was a reaction, I guess. Two of our friends were wiped out in a car smash this year. Outside Addis when the trucks break down – which they frequently do – the drivers leave them there with a trail of branches as a warning along the road. Tom and Irene didn't see them. They ploughed right into the back of a broken-down truck. We'd all been at this lodge out of town for the night and they'd left early. Laila and I found them the next morning. After that – I know there's no correlation – we thought it was time to consolidate.'

His voice faded and I couldn't help thinking of poor Tom and Irene who'd been hoovered up into Adam's history. He breathed in roughly.

'There are no greys over there. Everything is black or white. Crazy things happen.'

'You must like it somehow,' I ventured. 'The *Indiana Jones* factor.'

'Not when it comes to seeing your friends' insides *mauled* by wild dogs.'

'I'm sorry. I didn't mean that.'

32

'Who the hell ever knows what you mean.'

He stood and moved to the sliding door looking out over the lake. A group of skiffs in a race tore down the nor'easter towards an orange buoy set in the water. Habit grown deep, we both watched the twin leaders setting off on a new tack, sails set beautifully. A fine-looking race. Tomorrow I might take out the two-man canoe.

'They thought Laila's brother was gay, you know. That's why she was really interested in meeting you. Her Mum is Italian and her father has a transport company. Apparently her brother Bisrat went to Milan to study and lost the plot. He's back at home now, working with her father. He married a gorgeous girl, you know. Utterly gorgeous. They're having a kid.'

I thought: poor sleepy-eyed boy wearing beauty's noose.

'Great, another success story. Maybe we should all marry and procreate.'

'It's all very well for you to sit on your perch. We are talking about a culture with a three-thousand-year-old history. Not a truckload of white bums in leather.'

'Are you saying that in three thousand years their culture has never produced a man who loved another man?'

Adam backed off. His head was framed by an old seventies photo that Mum had blown up. It was Adam and I with floppy haircuts and BMX bikes.

'You know nothing of humanity,' he said. 'You're a sick bugger.'

After the film, the long sandy-skinned return of the couple from the beach, and Mum and Hadley's emptying of a couple of *pinot grigio* bottles by the water, most of the party were senseless. Adam, wearing a different Coptic shirt, saw Laila to the end of the lawn and she headed down the steps with a torch. He turned back to me. It was apology time, his eyes looked contrite. He grabbed my shoulder and squeezed. In my mind, I released him from the torment of the baking dunes and he wandered back to the oasis.

Mum and Hadley were expiring in front of the television. It was a documentary about deforestation in Africa, now part of their extended neighbourhood. I went outside down to the water, treading onto the jetty. Sounds travelled all the way across the black-skinned lake. I heard the bikie gangs on the other side with their kero lanterns and beers. Someone called out, *Bob! Where the fuck is Karen?* The lights in the boat shed were out. I started moving along the waterfront until I heard Adam's voice and stopped still. It was coming from the patch of grass below the Banks' house, down by the water. He and Leanne Banks were talking in the dark.

' – when he refused to stop, I left him. Not before he lost his job and raided our savings. He used to lay into Kyle.'

'You told the police all of this?'

I slipped behind Banks' boat shed and leant against the rock. I could just see Leanne open a couple of beers and hand one to my brother's back. The bottles chinked.

'Ellen told Deidre you're tying the knot,' said Leanne. 'Now, that's a new development. I never thought you'd get around to it.'

'Deidre told Ellen you're with a Maori guy. And he's younger than you.'

'Eight years younger. Come on Adam, you're not jealous?'

'You'd better keep him out of Jim's radius. He likes a bit of colour.'

'Oh, you can talk,' she said, laughing loudly. 'What about your *Ethiopian*?'

Adam didn't answer her. I waited.

'Hey,' he said in a lower voice. 'Why don't you turn over and let me see that arse of yours in the moonlight?'

A trawler gurgled across the lake with its triad of light.

White at the top, red on the port side, the starboard green. When the wash passed I couldn't hear them clearly. I heard her voice further back, suppressed, but couldn't make out what she was saying. Often, you can recognise the very last wave of a high tide as if it were tagged pink. After which the drive of the motion works on a different torque. I twisted upward and saw a cigarette lighter flare under the fig tree way up on Banks' wooden veranda and my back prickled. For a while the cigarette burned against the massive tree five metres above us. I hoped it was Deidre out smoking, or Leanne's oldest kid with a joint. Then I heard them moaning. I slid deeper between the old man's boat shed and the sandstone cliff until my body was jammed against the rock and I could just see them. My brother's white haunches were gaining rhythm over her and her fingers clutched the grass. Then I heard feet jangling down the metal steps old Banks had sunken into the stone and a huge coffee-coloured hand the same as Ruben's threw the cigarette into the ferns at my feet. He hauled Adam off as the screaming woman rolled over covering her face. The tall Maori kneed Adam in the groin and began to sock his jaw.

Laila came to watch me pull the canoe out of the boat shed. She smelled of coffee and bruised sleep. She asked if she could come out with me. I asked if she could swim. This canoe, handcrafted wood that I had sanded down myself, was an unsteady thing you had to keep moving, that a deep trawler wake could easily capsize.

'I think I'd prefer a life-jacket,' she said.

The sun was ruthless and narrow-eyed through muslin, which meant that tomorrow or the day after it would rain. Today was a day to nail.

'Then help me put her out.'

She wore her white bikini alone under the life-jacket, she wasn't interested in covering herself from me. Her hair settled on her shoulders though she ran one hand through it, revealing an odd gold earring hanging from the top curve of her ear. She turned around smiling.

We paddled off to the east as the light pooled on either side of us in heavy globules. There was no wind, just gassy mirrors of the sheer cloud. A couple of trawlers were crossing back with their nets hauled up high. Though I gave her an oar, she merely dipped it from side to side and let me do the rowing. Eventually she stopped, settling the oar across her thighs on the boat rims. I pulled hard into the roil and felt the schema of my shoulders, like a kit put together well. I might have stood a chance against the Kiwi last night, but I stayed sandwiched between the boat shed and the cliff, breathing lichen while Adam's head twisted on his neck.

There being no resistance we arrived at the beach along the promontory on the other side and I asked Laila if she wanted to get out. We slew into the shallows and I hoisted up without letting the hull scratch, though the rocking made her tense. I helped her off before beaching, then tied the bow to a rock I threw in from the shore. There was much scraggly bush cover, burnt grass, old fires and crushed cans. At Christmas and Easter water-skiing families camped here, burning up and down the smooth water on wakeboards behind boats called *Maverick* or *4-Play*. But this morning there was no one, just embers and the vague smell of shit. We had to cross back before the nor'easter churned up the surface. Far off, on another arm of the lake, the Dora Creek coal stacks released cords of smoke towards the faded mountains.

Laila hunched by the edge of the water on a strip of sand. Her thighs were dimpled, she hugged her knees. A fringe of pubic hair escaped coverage deep between her legs and made me feel fonder of her. I lay out, elbows dug into the sand.

'You've never made it to Addis,' she chided, leaning into the final 's'.

'No. Though I visited Adam in Nairobi. That was a long

36

while back. He'd been trying to sort out the office in Mogadishu and I turned up in the mayhem.'

'I've never been to Nairobi. Although my father had offices in Hargeisa in northern Somalia prior to the war.'

'So how did you guys meet?' I asked.

'It was through my sister, really. I don't suppose Adam told you. *Iri*. Irene.'

'No.' But the name snagged.

'Adam had been so close to our family. They were to be married.'

'What happened?'

Laila looked downward. 'Tomas is a German. She is expecting his child. Iri is the woman your brother wanted.'

I paused for a moment, thinking of what Adam had said yesterday. 'You mean they are still in Addis?'

'They were married yesterday in Addis Ababa.'

Laila slowed, she made sure she caught my eyes now. 'Iri did care for Adam,' she said. 'And I have always admired your brother. We are not bad people.'

She allowed me to watch her sad, yellowy face. Tom and Irene. *Tomas and Iri*. The couple Adam had slaughtered in the car wreck in his head. His beloved bearing another man's child mauled by wild dogs. And now Adam himself, the escapee flailing in the desert with his vile secret, his tongue bursting in his mouth. Laila turned to the other side of the lake where you could just make out the boat shed where Adam lay asleep on a leaking ice pack, his jaw wired, stitches in his chin.

'I am very glad to have met you,' she said, as the wind rose in oily scented puffs.

INFECTION

Princestown, April

Another pointless day, Ellis. They won't have the girl moved into a clinic. She's clearly suffering and should be on morphine now. In the mornings they lay her on a foam mattress on two tables pushed together; even so as they bundle her up you worry a bone will simply push through the skin. Just this morning before I left town - I can't bear Mother's gruelling prayer efforts any longer - I paused on her face and her eyes like a pair of spoons divulged a painful glow.

Eugene washed down the gauzy bread with a searing cup of instant coffee. Breakfast in the hinterlands of West Africa. His eyes strayed around the bar. Four plywood walls and a bamboo-clad ceiling, posters for competing national beers. The waitress sashayed out through plastic streamers nailed over a door frame. Five years down the road and she might look like Becky at home – a frail assembly of limbs, her organs kernels without an orbit.

He paid then headed back onto the sandy street. A way off was the beach. Last night he had heard a king tide booming against the small headland holding the fort. The massive sock of two heavyweights ramming shoulders. Wave versus sediment. Seas versus earth. Maybe the Prussians had listened to the same collision as they lay perspiring in netted beds. Hadn't they erected the minor fort before it passed to the Dutch? Two centuries before Wilberforce deplored the trade in slaves along the coast? The whips, the cassocks, the brass. And all for what? Tit for tat between Europe's restless third-born sons, the empire-builders and crackpots. And then Bismarck's tailspinning thrust that fractured the deserts, the quiet rivers and villages, the colossal forests with their soaring primordial virginity.

There had been chatter last night at the fort. Two women

speaking English had arrived carrying large knapsacks down the narrow hall. They had settled. Not without opening his lockless door looking for the bathroom and making the standard exclamations upon discovering the tap was dry. The generator had long ceased its putter. One knocked on his door and asked if they could borrow, or well, *have*, a match. Wide awake, he lit his own candle, then threw over a lighter. He saw the usual type of African adventuress. Apologetic, too smiley, a printed headscarf. She said they had a bottle of whisky if he'd like to join. Eugene declined. He blew on the candle, turning back to the sea.

Sleepless, his skin was a mask of sweat, suctioned into the hollow before each wave propelled its mass against the rock. Each boom worked upon his subconscious with a ravenous deconstruction, leaving palpable rivulets in the wake of the breeze.

It must have driven them insane.

Princestown, the day after

Occasionally, Ellis, you will see a trunk of implausible hugeness leashed onto a little truck. They come down from the forests. But if you look around the coastline you will see only scarred hillocks and rusted towns. People appear sodden, unwoken. As if the pillage happened yesterday.

Mother says Becky is lagging. I am half-inclined to catch a bus home - the old puppet strings - though the moment she pronounces the words 'The Lord' I steer townward for a beer. Apparently your hero Klaus Kinski filmed an epic here in the eighties. Oh, they say he's left a heathen litter somewhere in the hills.

The two Western girls were on the beach. The sun focused hard and sharp upon their translucent flesh and souvenir white-girl cornrows. A knot of kids swarmed around them.

Eugene would have liked to turn back but there was nowhere, really, to go. The town's fruitless streets he had combed in the hour after arrival, plagued by the same knot of ragamuffins. Seeking architectural delights he had found none beyond the auspicious fort, which worked no magic upon him.

That was it then, a confrontation was in order. They had already glanced in his direction, perhaps glad for respite from the youngsters. They oiled each other's backs, each round-shouldered, cupping pale breasts. One pulled on a baseball cap whilst the other merely closed her eyes, laying back, mistress of the sun.

It was not long before an irritation seized him. They were - what? Volunteers? Drumming students? Lain out like models on location. Ellis called it the *black beetle in his bonnet*. That once-removed sense of historical propriety that coursed his Camden veins. For in truth he had only been born and brutalised here.

Old Florence had given birth twice at a distance of eleven years. That was where his history began. After Independence Florence Ohima Boakye served drinks at the state lawn tennis club. The lithe politicians of the new regime exercised there, perfect as Englishmen, but brown and proud to the marrow. They were tall, heavy-jawed, now free to eat *banku* and *kenke* and *fufu* with their hands, fingers red with palm oil, eyes bright with local beer. They had waited, they had taken back their world. In one month three of the girls fell pregnant. By the time Florence's stomach was stretched, her breasts already leaking the cream she would feed her first baby, the President was in exile and her lover had fled to a village on the plateau. In a pink fairy floss dress altered along the seams Florence appealed to her lover's family matriarch. Her son was passed down the name he wore like a troubled conscience, given the old man could be bought for the cheapest fire-water to be had.

But Eugene's sister Becky was construed out of the

bitterness of the harsh years afterwards. She received no education, cursory love, much admonishment. She had a village girl's far-reaching submission, the stray dog's art of subsistence. Dark as charcoal while Eugene was pearly brown, she pooled their mother's wretchedness. Eugene, the family emissary, was propelled back to the first world where he wore his pelt like a suit from the back of the wardrobe. For years he was launched back and forth, from the world of tin to the world of glass. And here he was now, a man with an elaborate, undeserved education, whilst his half-sister's brain was nibbled by disease.

He trudged towards them. The first girl spoke with a strong Australian accent.

'You were at the fort last night, weren't you? Sorry if we disturbed you.'

Well, he thought, *I hardly expected to catch a bus along the coast without stumbling across your type.*

'You a Brit?' she asked.

'Looks like you've blown my cover.'

Joint laughter.

'A family visit,' he said.

'Well, we're drug runners posing as volunteers.'

'Of course.'

Eugene saw a coconut boy pushing a barrow up over the last drift of sand before the motionless town. He put his fingers to his lips and let out a whistle. The boy turned back, grabbing his cutlass and one of the green spheres. He began to run towards them as if his life depended upon it.

'Yessum massa!'

'Cut the massa and just open the coconut.'

Eugene saw the pale velvet of the boy's open palm, criss-crossed with wounds, one moist and beaded, before the blade raced through matter.

Princestown, night

The evening comes fast and close here, Ellis. The damp is pervasive, despite the sea breeze. The trousers I left on the chair still have not dried completely. The caretaker is a crafty man built like a bullock, who turns into an injured boy the moment the foreigners come for the slave tour. Greek tragedy from the descendent of qualmless Fante merchants, the stink of dirty history.

He drank with the two girls on the rooftop of the sea fort. The moon was in the wrong place, shedding no light upon the ocean. Wind sent the palm leaves slicing together. A child replenished their drinks with lukewarm bottles of STAR beer, rather than the CLUB Eugene preferred. The girls wore shapeless dresses, one with a tattoo like a bicycle chain around her loose bicep.

It turned out that they were volunteers working for a British non-governmental organisation, and were based at a hilltop town near Kumasi, a town the mining trucks and loggers hurtled through. There was little work beyond these two areas, and myriads of children. The girls taught the blind ones amongst these in an isolated school.

The Australian, quite a talker, soon took the centre stage. Whenever he frequented Westerners on his visits he had to listen to their stories of *living in Africa*, inevitably laced with condescension veiled as enchantment, and episodes of hapless gore. Eugene opened another beer as they spoke and his thoughts began to rove.

Despite old Florence's efforts to pitch brother and sister apart their shared blood had pulsed together. It was an uncommon animal, crossing over at will, plunging into the current of the other. If he had touched Becky in his room - the night folded over them - he had touched the unopened flower grown from his very skin. He hadn't wanted, not that. Becky had crept down his trunk on all fours, ass in the air, until her mouth had soothed him. If he had extended his hand, gliding over her, it had been to borrow back the heat they were melded with.

'You're not mad, are you?' It was the Australian reeling him in. 'That we're pulling this place to bits?'

'Not at all,' he said. 'I don't exactly live here.'

He might have wandered off to his room but there the dampness and the tossing of the waves were repellent. It was better here in the dark, with beer, with wind. The window started banging in his mind. *Why did Becky, who barely knew how to put pen to paper, ever write to him?* He knew it was her heart crying, for he too had cried when he had read the words, when the final blood tests confirmed, when her pitch down the earth's unremitting slope began a year ago. The window slammed. He saw Ellis perusing the letter, growing rigid at the exact terminology, the forbidden tenderness between brother and sister. Her convulsive stare at him. He wouldn't shut the window now, he knew he would drink on to deaden the slamming.

A whisky bottle appeared on the table with three cloudy glasses. He was handed a drink.

'Hey, lighten up,' said the Australian. She was frowning, considering him. 'Nobody said you did it.'

She began to talk again and now he listened. 'I had this kid in my class last year. Real little runt, the last of the litter. He wasn't blind at all, we only realised it right at the end. He could *see*, you see. Apparently he had malaria for the thousandth time and was in a coma for a while. When he woke up they thought he was blind. Malaria and too much chloroquine can do that. The parents sent him to us. I guess he thought he'd be on a good thing at the blind school.'

'Go on,' said Eugene.

'Well, it lasted months. He did really, *really* well. I mean, nobody doubted this kid was blind. He was slight and agile, but

44

he'd worked out he had to move with caution and occasionally bump into things. Which he did. I swear he caught the same corner on my desk every time he passed. Things like that. And I have seen blind kids - blind from birth. He must have studied them like mad.'

She took a swig of whisky. Eugene watched her throat, her armpits with damp, frizzled hair.

'I guess he cracked, he couldn't contain himself. They found him kicking a ball against a wall out the back. It was one of the gardeners. He tried acting blind again but it just wouldn't work.'

The other girl laughed a little but Eugene caved in. For the entire course of his education he too had been a brilliant actor. Once he found his place he had called upon every possible skill to offset the display of his colour. He too had walked full-on into objects he could see. At times he'd feared his soul would burst through his skin.

'What happened to the boy?'

'The parents came. They were so afraid we would think they had put him up to it. The father took him home and beat him.'

'How do you know that?'

'I went there. The kid was really beaten up. They weren't even going to send him back to regular school. And I knew if I gave them the money for the fees it would go to drink or debt-repaying or cloth for the wife. So I found a job for him at our school. Just arranging the desks and benches so the kids didn't trip all over the place. He only came once. With the longest face you've ever seen on a child.'

She rose from the chair. He watched her shoulder bones move under the skin.

'Look at Marion, will you? Snoring away again.'

Her friend arose in a splutter as her glass cracked on cement. Her eyes were those of a woken cat.

45

'Was I snoring? *Was I?*'

'Go to bed Marion, you're out of it.'

Marion obediently dragged herself away. Her friend brought out a joint which they smoked on the wind. It was strong hash, similar to the type Ellis kept in a set of Thai boxes on her desk. Eugene felt the window banging but it was now coming from a remote room that would require an immense effort to reach. The story of the blind boy had opened a path to the other girl, a path of worn earth and familiar bushes.

'So what are you *really* doing here? You can't just be wandering about.' She turned to him, her face unguarded.

But he wasn't ready to speak of that. 'You should help out the boy,' he said.

'For Christ's sake, he is ten and last I heard they had sent him into the bush with the loggers. I never even got through to him.'

'True. But then again, why should you? For him you are everything that he is not.'

'Yes, I know.' These were bare, cool words. 'I don't really like this place,' she went on. 'The deference, the kow-towing. Never knowing what people are saying or thinking.'

'You are free to go.'

'Thanks, that's a useful comment.'

'Personally,' he said this as he dragged deep on the next tightly-folded joint. 'I think all of you people should be kicked out. No foreigners, no foreign input, no IT, no courses, no funding, no food aid and no fucking experts.'

'What – so you want it to be like before? At Independence? When they managed to dismantle a functioning economy in five years? Where before they produced everything from aspirins to cars in this country?'

A photo of his father on a pre-Independence tennis court, racquet gliding. He heaved. But she was only partly right. Yes, old Florence had been taken in and implanted. And here was he, living seed of the colossal failure of the new nation. But there was more to it. Their leader. The ideals. The *love*. They had existed. And the implosion that came afterwards: the colonials had wanted it that way. Surely they had stepped back and nudged elbows at each collapse.

'And then what?' she continued. 'Leave it to the chiefs who've sold off most of the land to the mining companies? Or your politicians and their trips abroad? Sorry, those old idealistic arguments don't hold anymore. You've been away too long.'

The air turned in salty arabesques around them. The joint eddied along his nerves but it was shaping into a down trip, full of cranks at his back and crawlies along his spine. He stretched his legs, feeling the brush of feathers on his head. Tomorrow morning he would be on the first bus to Sekondi.

'You know, your Western enhancement is just a raft out here,' he said, enjoying the words. 'Makes little boys pretend to be blind.'

He pissed over the parapet while she was silent. Later, he led her along the narrow wooden hallway built for smaller men. She closed the door, leaned with a heaviness against it, watching him undress and part the netting. She pulled off her clothing in ragged movements but that was all he saw. For he had lain out, turning inward. She climbed onto his broad back and he turned he rose he lubricated her swiftly pushing her to the bed. Then emptied into her, demons on his breath.

Sekondi, April

She cannot be moved at all now. Mother said a group of them – her personal stray cats – prayed all night through Tuesday until dawn. Apparently she sat up on the bench early that morning and asked for MILO. She drank a cup, then the crackle ceased and she fell back into a coma. I have called a doctor friend at the hospital, even for pethidine I would inject myself, but he dissuaded me. Let sleeping dogs lie, he said.

47

My mother believes she can be cured.

Florence lived in an airy litter of rooms. Drawing room, parlour and salon were peopled with extended family members, their extended family members, the ailing, the poor, the good-for-nothing. The gallant colonial house wore broken curtainless windows with rusted grills attached on the lower level, presumably against theft. Stucco ornament, where not fallen away, was traced with the soot of decades and the house name resisted in cast concrete capitals above the front door, along with the construction date. Two worn lions either side with their burnished, dimpled stone mostly wore drying briefs, shreds of cloth and martyred T-shirts.

Far back in the house, Florence's private apostles prepared for her morning ablutions. Christian prayer came first, then exercise (she walked for ten minutes on an antiquated jogging machine, *for yes, she had been in the West*), then bread and tea. Florence dressed with aplomb. An array of cloth-sellers knew of her predilection for orange, magenta and aquatic green. Her seamstresses were constantly on call.

In the afternoons Florence banished the girls, sat on the bed nibbling groundnut and roast plantain, cast back on pillows watching an American soap opera with its furry yellow profiles, her dusty religious icons around her. After several days of absence she expected Eugene home today. At her core she knew her son was bound to her, that she had culled him from the universe and given birth. No matter that the father had been a scoundrel, that amongst his two dozen children he barely remembered Eugene's face and knew nothing of his countenance.

At the end of the day Eugene brought a pot of tea and sat with her. She began to admonish the small boy in him.

'Where have you been for so many days? The girl is surely going.'

He circled the room. A tall man in unwashed jeans and an old black T-shirt. His beard had grown. His hair needed combing.

'And what of your face and hair? You must *comb*.'

He sat down on her bed, his most open and reliable mark of affection, loosening his shoulders.

'You are not eating well.'

'Mother,' he said, and straightened. 'Becky is in the courtyard. There are flies sitting on her, noise, children flying past. Why don't you put her in the clinic? Doctor Rabel will take her.'

'They cannot help her. The medicine will not turn this thing backwards.'

'Mother. It's for the pain. If it's the money – '

'You think I have no *money*? Who looks after this house? Who has bonds in the bank? Who has put you where you are so that you could make a mess of yourself?'

'At least inside then. In here with you, or in my room.'

'She will bring death into this house.'

He versed her a scalding cup of black brew and stirred sugar into his own.

'Mother, it is even unhealthy to have her out there, amongst people who may not know.'

'They know she has been cursed, that is enough.' Then darkly, face sagging to the side, she said: '*Do you think there have not been others, skin and bone like starved dogs?*'

Eugene rose, walked to the low window ledge and sat down. Outside the neighbourhood fell to coves of tin under the dusk. Kerosene lamps smouldered the marchers home and the smack of *kelewele* frying in palm oil hit his nostrils. The old lighthouse began sweeping the sky.

'You will eat *kelewele*?' she asked. One of the skerricky girls was summoned, coins counted on the dresser. She returned with two wads of newspaper, the oil mottled through.

49

'There was young Beatrice across the road, you won't remember her.'

But Eugene did. A fair girl with beautiful, linear breasts.

'They say it is a question of time and Mary Quaye was forced to follow the same behaviour. I am not stupid. I know the cloth and bedding must be burnt.'

Eugene hurtled out of the room. She shouted to him – twice, three times – her hard voice starting to crack. She cursed the young girl who appeared in fright, whom Eugene whipped past. He tore outside through the layabouts on the steps. They were cousins of his decked like Bronx hoods. He rounded the flank of the house to where the two tables were pushed together, to where his sister lay arranged under the most consumed cloth.

It was so quiet. *She* was so quiet. He stood there, his breath thundering still. So many times he had watched her sleep. Entered her little side room when he came in piss-blind with *pito* after a night with old mates. He would check on her, touch her cheek or back. If he were conscious enough he would wait there until her scent entered his lungs a little. Maybe talk to her or make the silly promises you did to a kid. Here, the sickness was never a surprise. A street woman would throw herself on the ground for you, part her legs and gulp you down deep inside of her. Becky had fossicked in the streets, mated in sheds, lounged on the dirty beach until boys took her behind the palms.

He would have been the same had he stayed here.

Hours later he pushed open the tattered iron gate of his mother's compound. He stood where he had stood as a boy, years ago, watching workers pour concrete across the whole yard. Trees encircled with grey icing. Channels leading both from the rear of the kitchen and the toilet block towards the back wall. Commandeering operations was his mother, grown wider and crankier with the birth of the soundless baby cocooned on her back. She snapped at the workers. They obeyed her in gusts, all thin-chested men who beat their wives at night.

He had been to Doctor Rabel's house directly. He had caught a taxi to the small bungalow near the university, bought the vial and needle in a matter of moments.

Now they were in his pocket, twitching.

They had covered Becky in wet towels. He stood watching for a while, maybe ten obstinate minutes as he tried to fabricate her pain. Her skin fiercely traced the contours of her skull. Her lips were parted, her eyes two lifeless planets on a sepulchral pull into blackness.

—, April

Ellis! She is gone! She was there last night but this morning the tables were tipped on their sides. A small girl used a scrubbing brush to soap them down.

But Mother insists she is not dead, that they have taken her in a taxi to see a healing priest in Sohum. Sohum! More humps on that landscape than on the moon, in a taxi with axles grating on the ground, Becky fevered and too pained to be touched! For what? To lie on the ground and be babbled over?

Last night I had the morphine, bought from Rabel, the needle, the fucking diamond in the night, and I did not send her downward, Ellis. I could not.

Eugene learnt of Becky's death the next afternoon. He was sitting in a chop bar down the road looking at a smoked tilapia filet in okra soup.

'Master Eugene. They say Becky is dead. You go come to the house.'

He sat back, pushing the food away. So she had ceased to breathe. Her limbs no wider than his forearms would chill without the passage of blood, her cells die off in drifts. Then the shut-down of every organ and the new masters racing in – *chill, worms* – replacing life's flurry.

51

Eugene paid and staggered into the street. There was a putrid paste in his mouth. He saw the tin walls and crudely printed advertisements with shocking lucidity. Was he relieved? Deep in his gut the roar wilted. He badly wanted to shit. He stood there, fists clenched, watched by people trailing past, his temples and armpits dry as he distilled his grief.

He paced downtown. The sun was high and damning, snagging on skin, snagging on metal. A boy with rippled scars on his cheeks drummed a dirge on a wooden shoebox. Eugene paused by one entrance of the covered town market. Massive sacks of onions passed as a herd on th̶̶̶̶̶̶ Eugene followed the last of them inside and was swallow whole.

His eyes adjusted. In here there was a patchwork of tin roofs. Light shafts fissured the shadow, levelling certain stands with a hyper-real kinetic. In places, the reds and yellows flamed on labels of hair products, tomato paste and tuna stacked in tiers, and the bright blood seeping from pigs' trotters in tubs appeared to combust. Further inward, the shadows themselves reeked. Of smoked fish, of gutted flesh, of earthen pots bruised by the sun. Voices shot out. There was the constant *Ago! Ago!* of the *kaya* girls pushing down alley-ways, matched by the bunkum wailed by ladies on the stands. Eugene turned this way, turned that. He saw parts of the market he had never wished to see. Chickens gurgled in cages, feathers thick in the air, while fly-strewn chicken parts sat in clumps on benches. Goats were tethered, wailing *nah!-nah!-nah!* Next to these the very dried and tanned leather now enwrapping their organs.

Eugene's throat convulsed. The healthy body when opened emanated a smell of wetness, of richness. He had once held a warm pig's heart dribbling in his hand. The blood running down his arm like treacle. It made his mind jump to Ellis, blood on her thighs, still wanting him. The blood on his cock he pulled from her, how it coloured the sink. He hardened. A boy came up to him, a half-dozen woollen hats safety-pinned to a jacket hanging from his shoulders, a mirror around his neck on a string. A tight-fisted *Ga* face with the gouge in the middle of the left cheek.

Eugene halted. Now he saw what had happened to Becky. He saw the dawn in the misty forest, the taxi dwarfed by massive trees. Two figures shouting now that the sick girl had begun to stiffen inside the car. Then the descent to Sohum: the trolley wheeled into the empty parking lot of the small hospital, the broad aching nurse.

His mother's only other offspring in the world, would he have to stay here? He had brushed away that thought before. Though she had implored him enough in the past. Found him work in a clinic where the girls could pull out of an eight-month pregnancy and return home emptied, where he once found a perfect discharged foetus in a toilet block. She had offered him property, her very best, reluctantly conceding that his *fiancée* could make a decent man of him. But that was before Becky fell sick. Before Becky spent a year becoming an arthritic, feeble nineteen-year-old in the skin of an ancient woman. Eugene had flown out here twice after her stirring, babyish letter. The first time there were fevers, the cough, a painful limp as an imperfection in her hip began to flower. Then, three weeks ago, they had told him she was close to the end, that her voice clung to the sound of his name. Eugene had dragged himself over the globe, still angry that the girl had crossed his skin, that their love had become the vile animal Ellis had seen. That she should die now gave him a poisoned freedom to reconfigure his life. To crawl out of the pit. To run so far.

He stopped walking. Someone would have been sent to search the town for him. They all knew where he wandered. He saw his mother, rallying her apostles for a final dirge, the large television flaring soundlessly. All and sundry at the house would anticipate the lavish funeral party: the fried chicken, soft drinks and live band; the new cloth to be bought now that the thin girl had died. He pulled away from the market and went to the port. There was a place he rarely frequented, a run-down customs building adapted to house the town's most notorious bar, owned by a conniving local and a conniving British national. The port with its loutish Eastern European crews had established the demand for fair blondes to alternate with what the environment provided, so the place heaved with Ukrainian hookers and perky half-breeds.

Eugene walked into the bar. He went down the freshly painted alley-way to pee. But not even recent renovation had altered the foamy piss-pot he stood looking into, hearing a woman's long letting go next door. When he walked out he saw that the two white girls from Princestown had taken his place at the bar. *Holy hell.* Too late to back out. The girl he had used to ease himself. Of course their eyes fell upon him. Eugene felt a bolt slide across his chest. His father's son. The two-bit drunkard, all cock and no balls.

'Hey, you pushermen find your way back to town?' he said, trying to laugh. He realised he had no memory of her body.

He turned around. *Fuck*, he didn't need this *judgement.* A crowd poured in from the street like a badly dressed bunch of extras. Sailors in skewiff caps, mixed girls with hair extensions and sharp eyes. And in front of him, these two.

'Look, my family thing. It just hit the fan,' he said. 'And I believe I'm on my way to becoming drunk.'

'They left you off the will back at the ranch?' said the Australian, a tricky little tattoo dissolved into her shoulder.

'My sister passed away this afternoon.'

'Oh, sorry. Sorry for joking. I really am.'

The grit left their faces and the Australian signalled for another round of drinks. He almost felt let off for the rocky sex.

'What happened?'

He paused. Out there in the big world no one knew.

Only Ellis.

'She had AIDS.'

The words left him, falling in the flat light. He felt the implied contagion, felt the sweat in a second skin along his flanks.

'Would you like to talk?'

'No.'

The music exploded loud and fuzzy as the DJ with a huge mop of dreads spun Alpha Blondy. The two white girls negotiated their way to the dance floor, ending up with two local louts. Eugene couldn't watch. He transferred his interest to a bunch of sailors being primed by the girls. He knew they were killing time as their cargo hulks filled with reeking cocoa pods at the port. When stowaways crept on board, these were the men who hunted them down like vermin, sliding their bullet-pierced bodies into the ocean as their ships moved across the tropics.

Eugene careered outside. In his back pocket he had a phone card. He walked into a small plywood communication centre with two impossibly smaller booths nailed up inside. He heaved, then wrote down Ellis' number for the guy. He began to pulse.

Ellis' number rang long. He envisioned the phone on her work desk, the dim light left on in the hall. She was out. He tried to imagine where she might be, strolling where, smelling what; wearing which summer dress revealing her nutty legs and a coaxing pair of sandals.

For a while he circled the neighbourhood of fishermen and layabouts and their slumbering offspring. But an hour later he was drawn back to the bar. In his absence it had filled rapidly with a sea of shorn, bobbing skulls fused at breast, chest, buttock, and an undercurrent of *ganja* and glue. Eugene pushed inside, stilled by his disconnection. He harboured Ellis within him. He had just wanted to tell her, to have it over with.

Back at the bar the Australian girl was ordering a beer.

Eugene sat down, gulping the dark local brew until it hit the juncture of his brain and spine. He felt the needling.

'Where'd you get to?' she asked.

'Phone call.'

'Oh.'

With no warm-up she hooked her arm around him. He hardened, smiled, sent a message to his tendons to loosen up. It must have looked awkward from the outside.

He was too awash with sentiment to react. Not sentiment towards her, just a cloud of emotion bellowing through him: Becky's ungovernable pain and ravaged body, Ellis like a dart in his back and the way his mother could pitch the very earth he walked upon. She climbed down from her stool and expanded her embrace. He remained pinned there, knowing that the West swoons to give, to behold, to conquer. But he didn't want this. Her palms travelled the length of his back to the cusp of his buttocks, leaving warm trails on his skin. He felt the contours of her front. Unwillingly, he inhaled her smell of sweetness, saw the fair hair plaited in rows.

He pulled away without seeing her face.

He swung around and elbowed towards the street, feeling the relief burst a hundredfold through him. But it was more than dodging the girl. For now he knew that it was over, the whole circle, that he could leave this place in peace. His life was over here and he would return to his anchor. He felt a current of fresh sea water pass through him, washing deftly back. Darling Ellis of the coaxing sandals. For a year ago she had left him. The very day she discovered Becky's soul-scorching letter of complicity and doom.

God help him, he burst, *how he wanted her back!*

Sekondi, May

We have buried her, Ellis. The rains came, rendering jolty and protracted the drive up to the plateau where Mother had chosen her resting place. Church cronies. White steeple, sandstone manned upward from the coast, the stained glass carefully shipped out.

But Becky's service was held on the just-laundered dust. Tarpaulins tethered out over the wailing rent-a-crowd in flourishing black frocks.

My Mother sat in ground-swelling silence.

It is over now. Those of us who were closest threw the traditional clots of earth onto her shiny casket. The crowd wrung its hands over the wretchedness of mortality, then turned as a tired beast back down the bushy path at a distance from the town, on a mountainside where there is a great, pleasant gulf of air.

STROMBOLI

I imagine Reece would think his plan is going like clockwork. I think this as I observe the volcanic island of Stromboli rising before our ferry. Broad and black-flanked, it appeared an hour ago as a smudge on the horizon. When Reece comes later I know he will squint through his camera eye. He will line up the breathing beauty, pulling the view into focus. I bunch my bags together before searching for Nilda, my employer, and our group. All the while I stare at the precarious border of houses along the island's coast.

'You are ready?'

Nilda never misses a chance to try out her English. In Naples, nudging her younger boyfriend, she joked that the holiday would be *almost* exclusively devoted to that purpose.

I ask myself how Reece will judge our odd group, now on deck viewing the volcano. Nilda's eight-year-old, Milena, my charge for the trip; Nilda's boyfriend Andrea, in Timberlands and a Lacoste polo shirt; Nilda herself, a thickening Milanese paediatrician who has been visiting this island since girlhood. It was Reece's idea that I look for a job with a rich family – not in England but in Italy where they have villas and swimming pools. Reece lived in Rome for a stretch when he was a kid. When the topic of holidays was brushed upon, Nilda mentioned they usually went to their villa on Stromboli, where in fact the love film of Roberto Rossellini and Ingrid Bergman was set. Reece, who is also a movie freak, was ecstatic. This week he is hiking in Corsica, where his bony feet in a pair of Birkenstocks will reach cliffs. For some reason he thinks Nilda will be fascinated when I reveal his existence (his father is an Ashanti chief who went to Cambridge, his mother a towering Canadian painter) and will throw open arms to him as an inspired guest.

Looking sideways at Nilda I'd put my bet on him

sleeping on the beach. With me, Nilda slides easily into that intimacy you share with foreigners who work for you, who you know don't really count. But she can also criticise the way I stack her plates.

We gather our bags on the jetty, in the breath of the volcano. Nilda attracts a couple of porters away from the other passengers. Their wooden movements comply with Nilda's abrupt orders and they activate like heavy-limbed dolls. In the residue of this, there are a couple of tart words for Milena, now dawdling on the planks. Milena's eyes narrow, converting to pre-pubescent fury. Fatherless, she hides herself behind a grimace and five or six more kilos than her short frame really needs. It is essential that she wins at games.

But Nilda doesn't give a fig. She laces her arm through Andrea's, quickly tasting his pale, corded ear. Her white dropped-waist dress clings to her trunk in the wind.

The jetty bisects the landscape. The landscape *is* the volcano. Nilda has told me that the volcano erupts every fifteen minutes. Like a bubbling, blue-smoking science project. But Nilda says it is a hiccough really, just a slick of lava running down a black chute to the sea. Spectacular to witness of course, although last summer a Japanese photographer went too close and, well, was last seen tumbling into the crater. This was what Nilda said while in one of her chirpy moods back in Milan. As I watered down her choked geraniums, as she puffed a Phillip Morris over Milan's dirty roofs.

Nilda's back anchors the light when she jerks around wearing Jackie Onassis glasses. So she will miss what comes next: a curl of smoke pushing away from the crust, soundless as growth, fraying and dissolving in much the same instant. She has turned to tell us to hurry, nothing more. At the end of the jetty a three-wheeled van is waiting.

Milena arrives last, her Benetton T-shirt wet with perspiration.

The vehicle trundles along the immediate coast with its less dramatic dimensions. A factory, road signs, directions to hotels. I ask myself how could there be room for all this ordinariness. Indeed, the spell of the volcano has passed. From here it is just a tangled slope of weeds.

After a bend there is a town above us straddling two hills. The more prominent settlement shows its tight clutch on a Catholic church. Houses overlap around it, in jostled circles cut by the streets. Even from this distance I can make out stucco and tiles, iron tracery. Milena, gunned against the window, pockets details like shiny washed shells.

'Have you been here before?'

I turn to Nilda's boyfriend, Andrea, who is wearing a pair of gold-framed Ray Bans. The pores on his cheeks are filling with sweat.

'Yes, of course,' he says. 'I know well dees island.'

The van halts at the end of a section of pocked stone wall. There is an invasive smell like pot-pourri and the driver dumps our bright, plastic-webbed bags onto the earth. The light pounces on them as we crawl out. Heat bites into our scalps.

'What do you mean leaving our affairs like that? I've paid you to carry them to the house! Carry them at once to the house!' says Nilda in nasal Milanese.

The old man's back turns away from us like an ancient, dwindled source of power. He tucks his body into the shoddy vanette, kinking his neck so his huge head doesn't graze the door frame.

'But are you joking?' he says as the engine starts its insect whine. *'Carry your own affairs city woman full of wind.'*

Nilda tosses out a couple of expletives but Andrea nooses her arm, tugging as she stands there gobsmacked. The vehicle putters back down the hill into the stinging silence and we pick up our bags and start along the trail into the bush.

The villa, ten minutes on, turns out to be smaller than I

61

imagined. I feel a slight deflation, possibly more for Reece's sake than myself. Reece has been so expectant, and so visual in his expectations. He will be counting on something more opulent, more Dolce e Gabbana. Instead there is something very weekender and skinflint about the house, despite its original relics. There is an upper storey with an iron-bellied terrace jutting over the courtyard. Bright pink bougainvillea flowers rove along the walls, negotiating wooden frets raised above an old table. Nilda opens the triple-locked front door as a gush of mildewy air escapes, eager as if it had been waiting.

What will Reece think? I move tentatively through the dusty, roused rooms. Downstairs there is a dining area with a warped table, and a tiled bedroom with iron bedsteads. Every so often ceramic ornaments have been fixed to the austere walls. Upstairs Nilda swats the floor repeatedly. It takes me a minute to deconstruct my initial fears: she is only killing cockroaches. When Nilda intercepts me on the stairs she hands me a rolled newspaper and broom. The rest of the afternoon is spent squashing cockroaches then sweeping up their gluggy shells in the dust.

Within a couple of days the general rhythm of the holiday has been settled. Around nine or so we have a communal breakfast. I wash some peaches and figs, and set the outside table. Nilda asks me if eating cornflakes might help her lose weight. She unpacks a supply of skimmed milk. At first there is a reciprocal quandary as to whether I can take a place at the table. A couple of times I snack in the kitchen, or wait for them to conclude, but it appears to bother Nilda more than the farce of being democratic.

After washing up (my job), and preparing Milena (ditto), we head for the beach. Five minutes away, the beach skirts a small inlet where yachts anchor for the night. But by mid-morning they have drifted away with their booty of princesses and moguls. The beach is bordered by a fringe of boutiques, the grounds of a hotel and a bar that becomes a disco at night. The volcano is visible from every angle. If I lie on my stomach I can time the intervals between eruptions. Nilda is right. A spool of smoke is released every fifteen minutes.

Nilda unties her blouson top and unzips her skirt. She pulls out a bottle of skin oil and an *Espresso* magazine with a booby number on the cover.

'This,' she says, pointing to her flab in her cheery, be-my-friend manner. 'In three days this be *abbronzato*.'

'Tanned,' I tell her. 'It will be tanned.'

In the days that follow, Andrea's white ears that Nilda often kisses change to a deepening brown colour. Since he's arrived, he's started to work gel into his feathery haircut and sometimes other woman look at him on the beach. Each time he swims he reapplies a handful from the tube in his bag. Nilda tells him not to wipe his hands on her towels, should she roll over and notice. Unafraid, her cloudy nipples take the edge off whatever she is saying, like a second kooky woman joining us.

Milena drags me to the bar to buy choc-dip ice creams. It is the type of tasteless, industrially-stamped ice cream that I don't like. She darts away from me to her new rich kid friends from the hotel. They get a hoot out of making faces at me through the barrier, then splashing into the blistery pool.

I tramp back to the beach where Nilda is flaked out tanning. I report Milena's running away, and how I am barred from entering the pool area by an aggressive Sicilian attendant. Nilda hoists herself up on her elbows and her nipples jiggle into place. Andrea brings his *Corriere della Sera* together with a bothered look.

'Just leave then, leave her to her own device – '

'May I go for a walk then? I'll meet you at the house for lunch.'

Nilda nods, catwalking her fingers along Andrea's thigh.

Ten minutes later I am hiking along a thin dusty road flanked by hostile foliage, which presumably follows the coast.

The noises of the beach are muffled. There are tracks from mopeds and vespas, the ones you hear in the night. Around the next inlet a village suddenly collects above the water, perhaps where the artistic flow of the island is concentrated. A wall mural is visible through an upstairs window left open, seeming to take in gulps of air. I see a beautiful naked woman cross a balcony. She looks at me.

There is a track leading to the water. I scramble down this, dislodging rocks. The beach is a narrow strip peopled with nudists.

I consider crawling back but the action seems to demand completion and I make myself walk through the bodies, throw out my towel and begin to take off my clothes. I sit down naked, pushing my butt into the rough stones.

Not three metres away a man's long brazen body turns to me. I had failed to notice him so close. We take stock of each other's bodies. His is the dry work of tendons – he is as brown as Reece with the same fallen knot below the stomach. The man's face reaches mine at the very moment his resemblance to Reece strikes a second blow. Is this possible? He has same short twisted dreads, the same wide sketched eyebrows and freckled nose. Now he is motioning, not to me but to the plastic-looking thing grown between his legs. He has come up hard and quick. I study his cock for instants before recoiling.

Turning over, I throw my T-shirt over my backside. I ignore him when he speaks. Then I put my hand under the fabric and feel that I am wet. I remove my hand and place it near a sea insect struggling over one of the volcanic rocks. It looks molecular, teetering, insistent.

Lunch preparation, originally my domain, is something Nilda decides she has a better hand for. She declares herself on a diet and each day deals out servings of salad and bowls of fresh fruit. Milena routinely refuses to eat. I am dying for some rice.

Andrea hides behind a newspaper. At the end of the meal I collect the plates. Nilda might dry, but more often will smoke on the porch, complaining about her daughter. This goes on until about three, when we retire to our darkened rooms for the siesta.

I never fall asleep. My mind dreams of Reece. I probe whatever he would find along my skin, within my clefts. My hands become his fingers and mouth. I freeze when Milena stirs. I lie motionless when Nilda and Andrea begin their romp upstairs. I go to the wide marble sink in the kitchen. I rinse my arms up to their sockets, I douse my face. Just outside the open window the volcano rambles down from the sky like a brown-backed robber in the garden. Why does it now seem discordant? Could it tug the unconscious mind, the way the moon influences a woman's body? Are all of us subject to its precarious pull?

The day before Reece is to arrive there is an accident. Milena falls on the rocks when she is exploring with her new friends and seriously injures her back. An hour later a helicopter comes to take her to the hospital at Lipari, the larger island several kilometres away. I sprint down to the beach with the few things Nilda has asked me to put together.

Nilda, under shock, no longer seems to recognise me. Andrea takes the garments. His arm closes around her. They mount the craft behind a stretcher showing the crest of Milena's brown hair. The helicopter lifts creating a fracas.

I return to the house alone. That evening I light a candle and buy a take-away pizza from the hotel. I watch the candle erode. Andrea calls briefly to say they will be flying Milena to Rome in a private plane for spinal surgery. He doesn't tell me whether I am to go home or wait for further news. I can hardly ask him if Reece can stay here. I put the phone down and close the shutters of the house.

I wake up realising that Reece's plan to spend a holiday at someone else's expense has gone like clockwork, more than either of us could have imagined. I set out to meet his ferry, the same one I had arrived on a week ago. I spot him immediately up on deck. He is one of the first to take in the spectacular view, his camera on his chest like the eye of Cyclops. We hug each other on the jetty.

'Fabulous, isn't it?' he exclaims, disbelieving as I was in those first moments. I wait before breaking the news about Milena. He does not seem surprised, he does not believe his plans have casualties.

We go upstairs to Nilda's bed where I pull down her sheets and stretch myself over Reece's body. Sometimes our sex starts out slowly, in tones of light and limbs Reece has tried to photograph. I remember this is Stromboli, the love island of Rossellini and Bergman. Reece hasn't reminded me yet, but I know this is what makes him so heated and distinct. He holds my face inches from his, keening into me.

We cradle, we leak on the flowering tiles. The unshuttered windows admit a breeze carrying the scent of rotting figs. Behind the house the volcano spills into the fields. Reece rises. Naked, he leans out on the window frame. He waits until one of the small puffs of smoke I have told him about is released. I wash in Nilda's bathroom, using her expensive body cream from France. He is still there when I come out with a towel to wipe small coagulating pools on the floor.

'Think we can go up?' He looks across at me, and for a disastrous moment I recognise the man from the nudist beach.

I tell him what Andrea has told me, about the bar beyond the village where expeditions to the summit begin, and how groups of tourists sleep up there overnight. Reece listens, his expression sharpening. Already I know he will take this on, that this is essential to his world experience. I start to sound vague to stopper my neediness. Reece frowns at me, looking involved.

All that first day Reece studies the facets of the volcano wherever we walk. I take him to the small bank and he withdraws some cash. We pass by the post office where he sends a postcard to his brother in Toronto. In the afternoon, I buy bread and pecorino and peaches at the supermarket. We open the bags of food at the house. The bread is coarse and white. Reece takes large bites which his jaws work through. Did he sleep with anyone in Corsica?

'They say the temperature drops at night time and advise we take some extra cover. Do you think we can borrow some of these?'

Upstairs, Reece has opened up Nilda's ordered linen cupboard. I suddenly feel a twist of guilt. Where are they now? I glance around at the elements of Nilda's interrupted life I have so neatly placed aside. Her silver jewellery, a Moschino belt and hand purse, the MoMA T-shirt she used to wear to breakfast. I am alarmed at the way I have so calmly erased their existences. I hand him a couple of camphor-smelling covers.

That afternoon, stroking me, Reece asks me to climb the volcano with him. I'm tired of hearing him harp on about the bloody volcano, and tell him so, thus the tiff I had promised myself to avoid finds a second leg to stand on. Reece strides off. I end up following him about the house, powerless. I watch him pour drinking water into two flasks he has found in a kitchen cupboard. He prepares rolls.

At six o'clock that evening we meet up with the local guide and a small group of tourists. Most of these are bronzed, blond Scandinavians and Germans who shake our hands vigorously. Reece tries to talk to one guy who backs off to his own group. He turns around to me, advising me to take my last leak at the bar.

We set out in single file through the long grass. For an hour or so the volcano is hidden from view. The hikers before and after us are silent. Occasionally, a muffled sentence is spoken, and receives a monosyllabic reply strange to our ears. Remembering Nilda's plot of land below on the coast, I think how the confines of our world have shifted in just an hour. The path steepens, and a sharp curve projects us into the open. The town is revealed brokenly from far, far above. Of the small grappling houses I can distinguish none resembling our own, and nothing of the life form of which we are a part.

The guide is a local hotshot who doesn't like to hang around. Several of the Germans – and Reece – are up to his nimble pace. I am overtaken as I try to catch my breath.

Reece whispers to me, 'You don't mind if I go on, do you?'

The next segment is crueller, distancing us further and further from the brittle coast. Our feet trample over the path, making the most of a few footholds on the ascents. I look back again to the hazy town and I feel like Lot's wife, turning to a civilisation burst into flames and dust. The large girl behind me treads on my heels. I scramble on, the breath a jab in my chest.

The final stage of the climb is the slowest and most difficult. Every step I take in the fine volcanic powder feels like a thwarted movement in a dream. The large girl has overtaken me, and now bears down on the boy in front. My eyes fix on her buttocks. Their pumping and sloshing promise the only stronghold should I fall.

The crest we ultimately reach is not the Fuji-style crater I had imagined. The black hillocks brink and drop undecidedly, forming a maze of paths all drawn to a chasm emitting smoke. A ridge above this descends to an acid green phosphorescence. Night has fallen in these last moments of the climb, so that when an orange fringe surges out with a long, blown roar, it marks the air for instants.

I lie on my belly above the crater, feeling the heat on my cheeks. I think of nothing. Most of our group is now spread along the rim in poses of awe or exhaustion. Some share bottles of water. Hungry, I open one of Reece's rolls.

Reece finds me. He is exhilarated, his face is sweating.

'There's a shower of sulphur with every eruption. A sample of First World War trench tactics.'

We lay out our blankets where the guide indicates. Reece returns to the crust but I bed down. I slide a little before my body moulds into the sifted ash.

Far into the night Reece wakes me up. The hands tapping my shoulder become part of a rapidly vanishing dream. I open my eyes to a camera lens twitching on a windbreaker, and then an unmarred spray of stars. It is cold, I think. Slowly, brokenly, my memory begins to form.

THE CLOCK TOWER

At a certain point Dominique Grace's life snagged on a clutch of rocks. His young wife died of a remote form of cancer that also rushed through the body of his son. Three weeks after the boy's lungs expired Dominique bought a first floor apartment perched over the life of a Brussels' street, with a not too melancholy view of rooftops and trees. He chose a modular building bereft of the *Jugendstil* tendrils netted over every other façade. He changed the family house-help because the old one, well, he had never liked her.

Dominique was conscious of setting forth on a new foot. That meant order, even in the slightest of things. He kept no photos and, while limiting his overtime hours to a minimum, he resisted the pull of quiet corners of the house and any of the type of music that might crack his mind. When he was at home he listened to his neighbours. Upstairs was a medical student called Sebastien Tempels, who played jazz and humped a squealing girl every Friday, Saturday and Sunday night. Downstairs was an Italian girl who fought with her Flemish boyfriend every other evening. Dominique bought a widescreen television set and placed it to the right of the central window, which framed the first neon emblems that pricked the late summer nights. He had rediscovered a delicate simplicity, he thought. He cooked.

Very soon, certain things about the new house-help disturbed him. He'd only met her briefly, assured by an office colleague that the girl was honest and reliable. The 'girl' had been hitting thirty-five or so, and had a low unattractive rear packed into a pair of bleached jeans. She was Chilean, without papers.

The first time Dominique found a long thick black hair on the bath tiles he felt sick. Babette had had silky medium-length hair she repeatedly tossed over her shoulder. Towards the end, the old house had whole balls of it along the parquet.

Dominique held up the hair, twisting the scales between his fingertips, feeling sandpaper at the back of his throat.

Then, regularly, Dominique began to find a pair of slippers, old embroidered espadrilles, tucked at the back of a hallstand he and Babette had bought together at the *marché aux puces*. He picked them up, smelt them, felt the contours pressed into the jute inside. Years ago, on a ferry sailing out from the Tuscan coast, an identical one had slipped off Babette's white foot. It made a *plish* into the green galloping waves, then faded from the surface. The couple had exchanged their alarm. Babette had removed the other slipper and tossed it with a fury towards the land. It knifed the air, scissoring and twirling and flipping behind a crest.

'Now I am your barefoot slave,' she had said.

Dominique threw the slippers out.

The first woman Dominique encountered after Babette's death was young, as he preferred, Flemish and vaguely arty. Arty, in Dominique's eyes, because she wore multiple studs in one ear lobe and a teasing black cross. It was about as far away from Babette as he thought he could go.

They met at a party. She was a consultant from his department who spent time in Africa and said she liked it. Dominique, who didn't wish to get to know her in excess, imagined her wearing awful printed dresses or arm-in-arm with a black. Accidentally, at first, his hand touched her breast when she was bumped from behind as he handed her a drink. It was the underside, the part that began its gentle cantilever away from the ribs. The girl looked at him tellingly. If Dominique began to sweat, it was with the relief of finding a completely unfamiliar body. It helped him smile at her.

The girl had drifted back to where he was standing as the party thinned out. In the car on the way home, she pointed out the clock tower of the Gare du Midi that she said was going to be knocked down the next day. Dominique ducked his head and saw blackness.

'You should go down and have a look at it before they destroy it,' she said. 'It's an Art Deco specimen. Somebody'll realise it in about twenty years from now.'

Her name was Toby.

The last straw with the house-help was the pair of briefs on the radiator in the bathroom. Lain to dry, he lifted the shimmer of purple stuff. It fell apart to reveal a faded menstrual stain on the gusset. Dominique, remembering Babette's ceaseless, corrosive haemorrhage, felt his innards clench.

He returned from work early on one of her afternoons and came up the steps quietly. The radio was jammed loud on one of the commercial stations. Dominique slotted in his key and stepped into the apartment. Flowers had been arranged in a vase on a spotless table; the carpet looked ruffled.

He found her at the end of the short hall, in the bathroom, hitting a brush against the sides of the toilet bowl. Her back froze as she sensed a presence behind her. She flicked up in a pathetic position of defence.

'Oh, it's you sir,' she said.

Water from the tips of her raised rubber gloves runnelled onto her jeans. Her face was flushed and her brilliant black eyes blinked at him.

Dominique began, 'I have a complaint, a slight complaint, to make to you. There have been articles of yours left about this apartment. It's not what I'd call appropriate.'

The forehead twinged. Something in her genetics had spared her a single line.

'I'm sorry. I don't know what you mean, sir.'

'I mean shoes. I mean your hair. I mean panties in the bathroom. Please.'

The face shot down, infused.

'Oh, the panties. Oh, I'm very sorry. I had a heavy day. I

had to rinse them out.'

After what Dominique hoped was a meaningful pause he went out to the kitchen where he reheated what was left in the coffee percolator in the microwave. It tasted old as he poured it into his chest. A half hour later when the 'girl' was paid and standing there in her denim jacket, Dominique said a stern good day. Then, from the window over the street, he watched her standing at the side of the road looking from left to right, again and again, waiting for the traffic to ease.

Dominique remained by the window over the flickering city. The next thing he would do would be to call Toby, the girl he had slept with. When he thought about it, Dominique called what they had done 'young' sex. There had been a lot of noise and several disarming positions. Though it shamed him, he was now used to the idea that he had had another woman. He held up the business card Toby had left, getting ready to speak. There was an answering service with the message in English, in Flemish and then in French, as was the way in this city. The English message said: *Hello, you've reached Toby Vlaminck but I've taken off again. I'll be in Ghana until November so I guess it's not worth leaving a message unless it's October twenty-something. Oh, and Didier's still with M.S.F. in Rwanda –*

The next morning Dominique walked downtown, intending to visit a couple of junk shops around the flea markets. He veered too far to the left and exited onto the parking ground of the Gare du Midi, where the food stalls were in full swing. He browsed a little. As he strolled a North African man gave him a dose of angry abuse for no good reason, which sent him wending into the tunnel under the railway with a wave of harmless-looking people.

In the light again, with the crowd dispersed into the station, he found himself alone in front of a chain-wire fence surrounding a good block or so of rubble. He stood there a few minutes, wondering how on earth he would get back. Then he realised that this had been the clock tower of the Gare du Midi that Toby had pointed out to him, that he had looked up for but had seen only blackness.

NATHALIE

The plane was held up in Lomé. Mona didn't bother leaving the house. She checked that Miguel was sleeping. He was: the slow fan wheeled above him, his hand clenched a shroud of mosquito netting which she loosened and let drop. She went out to smoke on the terrace, the city air a giant belch of open sewers and fried food, a gassy decomposition. Mona had seen travellers gag at the channels of waste snaking through the city. Where old women straddled and pissed, where a fallen coin might well have plopped into magma. But for her it was the most acute of honesties, the travails of the city were naked.

Nathalie called again and Mona's stomach eased. The plane had landed, she sounded intact. Frankly, Mona was relieved she would not have to spend the night visualising local technicians fingering the plane's entrails on the tarmac. She could sleep. From the liveliness in Nathalie's voice she must have met some fellow traveller on the flight and shared the wait. Envy flickered. The only people who talked to Mona on planes were women as chiselled as herself. They were a robust tribe, nationless and colourless, they made lean talk.

She parked in the new car park and shushed away the watchmen closing around her. She pointed at a bright-faced one and the others slouched away. She strode up to the dense triptych of the airport entrance and recognised her daughter to one side talking to a tall man, a returnee she ventured.

'*Maman!*' Nathalie broke free, nestled her face in Mona's neck, the shameless child who used to sit on her belly and tweak her nipples. '*Tout va bien pour toi? Et Miguel?* Is he asleep at the house?' She placed her cheek against Mona's, her skin still so soft, a loving gesture.

'This is Seth, *Maman*. His family is from here. He's working in Paris too. He is here to do some work up north.'

Nathalie made space for Seth's long arm to wend out and their hands shook. Mona's thoughts: edgy, cool, burning for success. They would sleep together before either of them flew out.

Seth had a ride coming in from Teshie, an aunt who was a nurse. He was fair, with a drop of milk in his skin and trendy thick-rimmed glasses. Mona was staring. Chaos surrounded them now. Another plane had released its passengers and they pushed as a many-headed mass through the glass doors as fakirs stormed towards them.

She wanted to take Nathalie home, to have her on the terrace sipping a mug of green tea. She tugged on Nathalie's arm.

'Miguel is alone,' she said.

'Of course! Seth, I'll call you tomorrow, *d'accord*? We'll most probably go to the beach, okay *Maman*?'

Mona took Nathalie's camera bag and pushed past the hustlers and vendors, down the steps and under the neem trees back to the car park. She didn't want Nathalie to see the tears that had sprung into her eyes. Her jealous tears. She had wanted Nathalie to herself.

In the car Nathalie chattered. 'I was so certain we would be catching a bus from Lomé! You have no idea how full the plane was until Abuja! I'd forgotten. It's been too long, hasn't it Mona? Just how have you been in your little house on the roof? Are they paying you properly in that silly school? Does your lover still visit you when Miguel has gone to sleep?'

She pinched Mona's side and Mona could feel the skin stretch. Months ago now, her lover had returned to his village when his young girlfriend died delivering twins. He had asked Mona for money and disappeared, leaving Mona feeling robbed.

'How long can you stay in town this time? You're not going to go north with that guy?' Mona said.

'Oh, *Maman*! He's a photographer. It will be good to work with someone else. He has funding, you see. He is working on a book.'

'What of Xavier?'

'It's over, Mona. I told you that. Don't make me go there again.' Nathalie spilled a knot of tobacco into a skin and rolled up fast. 'Here Mona, take a drag on this.'

Mona inhaled. It rushed across into her blood.

'How is that little monkey, Miguel? Is he still your sweetbread?'

The truth was that Miguel was a challenge. He had the same flints in his eyes as his father. He was disobedient. He loved to trick her, lie to her. Mona began to cry in the dark.

'Oh, *choux*!' Nathalie touched her hair, smoothed her neck. 'Don't cry, *Maman*. It will be okay. I've missed you so hard. Now we will be together.'

They brought her bags up the damp concrete stairwell to Mona's haven at the top. Four rooms, a detached shower and washroom, the apartment was an afterthought on top of the block, with broad views from the blurred sea line to the horizon of cheap cement houses spotting the scrub. But it provided the sky at all hours, in all her moods. Mona prepared tea while Nathalie tickled Miguel in bed. Later they sat out there in silence, Mona having forgotten all she had wished to say to her.

Miguel charged into her room and wriggled under the thin sheet. Mona had put Nathalie in her studio, where there was a spare mattress propped behind her easels. Last year Nathalie had brought her new boyfriend Xavier with her and they'd been intertwined, interchangeable, every comment and glance. Mona, whose loves had been unequal and endured, adored their complicity. But something had erased what had thrived between them. Nathalie had moved on and Xavier was a thing of the past.

Miguel pinched her soft stomach. 'This is my home, *Maman*! My old house! Wake up so we can go to the beach!'

She felt his wet breathing on her neck. The two of them, Nathalie and Miguel, were the only ones who still identified the parts of her body. Her used breasts, her shrunken womb, her thickening middle.

'Get off me, Miguel. You're too hot.'

She was surprised to see Nathalie in the kitchen in a T-shirt and shorts, her city skin so pale.

'*Bonjour Maman!* I've just called Seth. You don't mind if he joins us at Kokrobitey? I know you will like him. Look! Here is your present. I brought you some tools and paints.'

Nathalie opened the box of Japanese tools and Mona saw knives for slicing through linoleum, scalpels for her buttery paintings. The gleaming tubes in a row.

'And I saw your work in the studio – just a little – you must show me afterwards. I am so happy to see you are working!'

In an hour they were deep in the sluggish traffic through Kaneshie, the market thronging, churchgoers pacing along the overhead bridge, mothers close to the kerb with dangling children sashed to their backs. If Mona painted here it was because at home she was constricted, she could hardly explore her compulsion. Here she had found colonial villas painted toothpaste blue, and flaking stucco archways and statues dappled with tiles. There were lopsided hotels over the Atlantic from the post-Independence years, with dry shattered swimming pools and perilous diving towers.

Mona worked hungrily. In the beginning, nobody but Nathalie knew. After school Miguel went downstairs to kick a football with the children from the block and she went into the hot little room with its ceiling fan and glass louvers rusted into place. She sketched, she worked from photographs. The young boxers in the square, their faces twisted masks. Children soaped along the fetid canal while in the background football players scrambled in the dust.

'Miguel, have you been looking after *Maman* for me?' Nathalie had asked her brother about the school teacher he detested, and before that about the dog downstairs that had disappeared. Of their two fathers, Miguel's had been more passionate, but crueller. He had grafted Mona onto his life when his partner had left him. Slowly, he had enthralled her, leached her, had almost stolen the child.

'Where is Xavier?' Miguel had asked.

'Xavier has gone back to his old girlfriend,' Nathalie finally revealed to them both. 'He's gone back to London.'

The road behind the beach huts was sandy and knotted with bumps. Mona's low Lada revved and laboured along the woven palm leaf fence on one side that marked out the private plots of the foreigners. Diplomats had started to upgrade the area with concrete weekenders fanning out from the coast, some with walls crenulated with broken glass and uniformed watchmen carrying batons. Mona had been lucky. She'd been handed down an unpretentious wooden hut by the cultural envoy at the embassy. He hadn't liked his successor and had offered it to her. Sitting at the end of the dirty sweep of beach, for the moment it was the last construction before the rocky point.

She pulled into a gap in the fence but there was a car parked in her spot, a little white Suzuki with churchgoers' stickers on the back window. The auntie from Teshie. Seth had borrowed a car. Mona looked around for him and there he was, stepping off the porch to greet them.

'Who's that?' said Miguel. 'There's someone in our house!'

'It's okay, Miguel. It's my friend Seth. He was on the plane with me from Paris.'

Nathalie hopped out quickly and they strode towards each other, exchanging kisses on the cheek. Miguel stared.

'Come on, Miguel,' Mona said. 'Help me with the bags.'

A shirtless villager rushed up behind the car. It was Jacob, their watchman, wearing a pair of Mona's old shorts with a woman's plaited leather belt. He opened the boot and brought Mona's cool box and baskets up the steps, fishing for the keys in his pocket.

'Hello again, Mona,' said Seth.

'Seth, this is my little brother Miguel,' Nathalie said, holding her brother's shoulders. 'Miguel, meet Seth.'

Miguel sized up the tall man with an impressive Leica on a strap around his neck. For years now Nathalie had no longer lived with them and her visits were short, exquisite eddies. The last time she and Xavier had left Miguel had shouted at Mona, he had screamed and sobbed at her on the terrace until he had crumpled into a chair and slept. Miguel turned away from the pair. He ran down onto the sand to play.

Briefly, Nathalie helped Mona unpack. But Jacob took over, flinging out the printed tablecloth and pegging it in the wind, putting out glasses and a jug of cool water immediately. After years in the employ of her high-ranking predecessors, Mona had failed to rewire his zest. Sometimes she sat back and was grateful for it. Twice, though she shrank to think of it now, she had paid Jacob to keep away. She had sent Miguel to a friend's house and had brought her lover here. The young man had waded into the thick night waves, beckoning her. She had thought of their bodies washed up in a putrid cove in the city.

Mona opened three bottles of beer. The surf frittered along the beach and the wind tugged her hair. Nathalie threw out her towel and sat down in her bikini. Seth watched her and gingerly lowered himself. As he crouched in the sand in his jeans and grey T-shirt, his heavy boots still laced, Mona became curious to see his body. She rotated him in her head, naked, seeing the long heavy thing and his tight high buttocks. She saw that Nathalie's body was lain out for him. Mona hadn't had that sort of youth. Love had come in taut trickles and then gone furling back. Men had come to her in defeat and moved onward. Even her lover, the way he had allowed her to photograph his body, the way he'd stilled before her, she had seen his imminent departure surfacing in his eyes.

Nathalie sat up and waved to her and Mona brought their beers onto the sand.

'*Tiens Maman*, sit here with us. The sun is so rich!' she exclaimed.

But Mona shook her head then returned to the little porch and drank alone. She watched Nathalie laugh. She saw her small hard breasts and flat stomach, her twitching thighs. Further away she looked at Miguel playing in the sand. Jacob walked down with his bucket and spade and helped the child dig. Other village kids raced up to the fair European to try to snatch his toys. They were dressed in rags with amulets around their necks to ward off the deadly spirits prowling the village. Jacob chased away their red furry heads.

After a while Nathalie trod back to the hut, sand stinging her feet. She tied on her sarong. She put sunblock on her arms and turned to Mona to smooth it into her back. Seth watched mother and daughter on the porch. He looked expectant. Mona felt a slither in her gut.

'We're going for a walk to the point, *Maman*. Seth wants me to show him what's on the other side and maybe take some shots. You'll watch his car, won't you? He says he has his camera stuff inside.'

Mona watched them walk away. When they were far enough, almost hidden behind a ledge, Mona saw their bodies hook together and share a probing kiss. Mona's eyesight was excellent.

Over an hour passed. Miguel and Jacob came back to the shade. Miguel was hungry. In the meantime Mona had bought baby barracuda from a pregnant girl with an aluminium basin on her head. To lower the tin the girl bent perfectly at the waist, her spine thrust straight out as the cumbersome belly dropped downward. Mona had seen this action over and over, and each time thought of how she would convey the extending vertebrae and the swaying breasts, the membrane harnessing the curled child. It would be hard to reproduce the kinetic. She too was hungry and had finished her second beer.

Jacob had lit a fire and now the coals were ready for grilling the fish. There they lay on the grey wood pallet with their slit bellies and numb eyes, just degrees away from life. Miguel had helped Jacob. He pushed the serrated knife deep into their slimy pouches, pulling the squidgy stuff out, watching the organs collapse in the sand.

Mona had begun to worry. The beer had a sour chemical taste. Everything was too warm and the wind had blown a veneer of grit over the table. She walked down to the water's edge, past the indentation Nathalie had left in the sand. She was wrong to fret. She paddled her feet, wishing she were the type of person to cast herself into the sea with abandon, to roll on the bottom and watch the waves from underneath. She wondered if this Seth were to be trusted, or if they were simply making love on the bed of a rock pool, the sea trailing over them, mouths cupped together.

Miguel shouted. She saw Jacob take off running. She looked to the point and saw Seth half-carrying, half-supporting her daughter down the rock shelf. Nathalie was limping, struggling with a knee, crying. There was blood on her thigh.

Mona gasped and began to run. As her throat dried to dust she had a quick *déjà vu*, indecipherable, merely an evil flare. Focusing as she ran, she saw that Seth looked as though a horrible poison had travelled through him, and his camera was gone. Mona saw Nathalie throw up on the sand.

Nathalie staggered into her arms, pushing away from Seth. Jacob stood transfixed, Miguel grasping his waist. Mona wanted to shield her son's eyes, wanted to censor another image burnt into his memory, *the day my sister was attacked on the rocks*. Mona couldn't look at her fully. The soiled body, the sarong sticking to the blood, the wet shapes of her thighs. Mona wanted to scream at Seth. Broken sounds fell from her mouth.

She held Nathalie close. 'What happened to you? Who did this?' She smelt the acid in Nathalie's sweat, saw there was a small cut on the side of her neck. 'Oh my baby!' she cried. 'Can you hear me?'

She began pulling Nathalie along. Nathalie sobbed with each step. Miguel held fast onto Jacob, who said something about the police. Seth strode along with them hard-faced and wordless.

When they reached the hut Seth dissolved. He climbed into his car and covered his face with his hands. Then he manoeuvred past Mona's car and drove off.

Mona ignored this and sat Nathalie in the rattan chair on the porch. She covered her scratched shoulders with a towel. Nathalie shook as the tears dried on her face. Jacob smothered the fire and began to pack their things.

'Miguel, help Jacob put the things in the car,' Mona said. 'I'm taking you to the hospital.'

'No.'

'Just tell me what happened.'

'Doesn't that seem rather obvious?' Nathalie said, turning on her. It wasn't the first time.

'Did he hurt you? Why didn't Seth do anything, for God's sake?'

'Oh shut up, Mona. Just shut up.'

Mona had had her first exhibition at the French Cultural Centre a month ago. Nathalie, filming a documentary in Berlin, had been unable to come. Mona had sold three etchings which a friend of hers framed. Two paintings were bought for inclusion at the Nungua Gallery, where a good deal of international tourists passed. Mona had received her first payments ever for her artwork. After so many dark years, it was a triumph.

But the image she adored most had to leave her. It had been inspired by her lover, just before he had disappeared. One

85

night Mona had taken out her camera. She began to photograph his body against the cool bathroom tiles, which was where they made love as Miguel slept. The canvas she had painted afterwards showed a man on hands and knees pretending to prowl, his spine hanging low between his rump and high shoulders, the genitals concealed. Not prey, not a hunter, but a harrowed mythic creature. When her lover left her soon after she finished, she knew the painting belonged to neither of them.

Mona drove past the gallery on their way to the clinic. Nathalie had agreed to see Mona's gynaecologist, an older Ivorian woman who ran a clinic on the outskirts of town. The doctor cleaned Nathalie's wounds, took a swab and blood sample, while Mona listened to her daughter release weak cries. Mona felt dizzy. When they were small she had wanted to absorb their pain, to steal their fevers into her own skin. But this, the idea of wanting it was ghastly.

'Have you gone to the police?' the doctor enquired.

'Well, no. My daughter didn't wish to.'

'Why on earth not? You don't think this is a crime? Were there any witnesses?'

There was Seth.

Nathalie called out from behind the screen. 'I'm not going to the police.'

'Well, I recommend you think about this happening to someone else. Some other woman like yourself. It makes for a very unpleasant experience.'

They drove home through the traffic, Nathalie staring ahead. Mona had left Miguel at a friend's for a few days, without saying why. It was beginning to feel as though she had brought this on, the walk with Seth to the point, the sickly kiss. Is that what Nathalie was thinking?

'I'll take you home then. Maybe you should get some rest.'

But she knew Nathalie would not. She knew the man's

smell would be there, the prick of the knife, the shocking organ steady.

'I'll make you a good cup of tea.'

They paced up the damp stairwell. Mona stumbled on the steps, grazed an elbow on the concrete wall, regained her balance. Up on the rooftop the evening wind channelled through the rooms. Nathalie walked directly out to the terrace and for a moment Mona worried she would cast her body over the rail. But she lowered herself onto a chair. She moved with pain, clutching her abdomen.

'Would you like a cover?'

Nathalie didn't answer. Mona brought out an old silky piece of *kente* cloth with rippling blues and golds. She tucked it around her. In the kitchen Mona prepared green tea and pulled down two cups. These actions made her feel useful again, as though a healing could begin. She thought of her art, she thought of Nathalie's love of her craft. They were strong women, they would overcome this awful day. Mona brought out tea.

But outside Nathalie looked so much older. The lines Mona had never noticed on her face had become grave and hard. Her eyelids were fallen, discoloured furrows below them, and the cheeks were those of a gaunt woman whose good health had been stolen. Mona was silent. Everything had been taken from them. This was the day that would never pass.

GORGEOUS EYES

A world famous photographer flew into our hotel to savour the native landscape. She was a harried, shrill-eyed nicotine addict who walked with a self-absorbed beat. I took an instant dislike to her. My wife did not.

The famous photographer rose early and traversed the breakfast salon to the pool terrace outside. Here she would draw deeply on French cigarettes and sip double espresso coffee. Food did not appear to interest her at this hour, although one of the girls – Mercy Obede – later claimed she saw her put bread rolls and a banana into deep khaki pockets. That first morning when I went out to greet her I saw she had cords stringing from her ears and the distracted, if sought-after, expression of one appreciating sophisticated music. I retreated inside. She walked out of the hotel doors with a bold step, ignorant of flashy doormen and prompt drivers, flexing through foliage towards the public taxi rank on the street.

I assume the woman went about her business in the chaotic town centre. Of West Africa's major cities, ours is one of the quieter, more tolerable postings. The day arrives suddenly, breaking in a display of liquid light on rowdy traffic and market ladies swaying downtown. Plant life is agile and the climate is tense. If left unchecked vines will arrest buildings; in a month a roadway will desiccate.

It is Mercy Obede who obtains a copy of the photographer's latest art book which I peruse. The woman is called Nina Cooke. She is a resident of no country, a claimant of no distinctive culture. For forty years she has prodded the world with her testy Hasselblad. She has consumed pigs' trotters, snake entrails and frothy palm wine with respectful relish; she has crossed deserts, shaken the hands of chiefs and war lords, and won distinguished prizes. In short, we are told, this woman has constructed an original, feisty life.

I turn the thick, perfectly grained pages. For the uninitiated, the first images show high-shouldered Dinka men – erotic in beaded body corsets – mustering cows on a stark landscape. Eye glances are expertly caught, sweat-greased limbs and buttocks poise alongside the mass of crimped horns, and the flux of an unknown world is revealed with skill. And yet for the seasoned watcher, born here, one who knows how these boys play soccer, wish for jobs, are balmy with discontent, the dying exotica becomes a crucible of sadness. I glance on, frowning. If Nina Cooke's gift ever needed an honest name it would be the invasive rebranding of humble detail. It appears she is at the vanguard of a vulgar world trait.

My wife Margaret enters my office as I close the photographer's book. She wears an electric, upheaved expression. Her eyes fall on the book's cover image – a Muslim desert woman whose private loss becomes jaded haute couture.

'Oh, darling! Have you met her already? Don't you think she's marvellous? I don't believe we've ever had anyone as culturally rich as her. She's devastating – such a *force*. She says she wants to photograph my eyes.'

'What?'

I am not an envious man by design, but the exploration of Margaret's eyes I feel is my exclusive right.

'My eyes, Olivier. Nina says I have gorgeous eyes. She wants to photograph them.'

I light a cigarette, considering Margaret. There are times when her naivety astounds me. A woman of fifty regresses terribly, she will fold into her girlhood with a possessed innocence. Several times, since her operation, Margaret has become infatuated with sultry men who ignore her.

'You'll have to charge her a fee,' I say, turning the thing on its head to quell my sudden, unreasonable anger.

'Whatever for? Are you joking? This woman is an artist.

90

This is a privilege, Olivier.'

I turn the book around to her. In her grasp it falls open on the page of a young Somali bride, modestly dressed, surrounded by pugnacious sisters.

'Do you see?' I say. 'This book is a glossy celebration of Africa's cruelty. That woman is about to be raped by her fifty-year-old groom. She has been circumcised by those women surrounding her. She will know pain for the rest of her life.'

My wife looks at me with horror. She shuts the book.

Mid-morning the following day Mercy Obede knocks at my office door. I am irritated by my own brooding mirrored in her eyes. She enquires whether I should like coffee or tea. Directly outside my window a gardener is severing a tall plant presently guarding my shoulder from the sharp sunlight. I unfasten the window to check the youth, but find the sliced, now bleeding protuberance a dozen centimetres short of my forearm. I shoo away Obede's ruptured face.

On my rounds of the hotel I find the usual fervour underway. Kwabena in the souvenir shop salutes me, handing me a fresh copy of *Le Monde*. In my hands it is still tinged with the metallic scent of air travel. At the reception desk three superb Ivorian girls answer telephones and direct shabby tourists to the coconut grove bar. Their synthetic plaits glint under the lights, painted fingernails skittering as they speak. At their backs on varnished wood, five stylised clocks announce the time in significant world cities.

For an instant I turn on my heel. I have seen Margaret heading towards the pool area holding a large hat and magazine. She walks along the tiles in a pair of flattering Italian clogs, wearing a silver anklet I haven't noticed before. Everything about her – her dreamy step, the expensive white shirt she has chosen – makes me think of her decline. The fans gasp in unison outside, blowing a gust over her body. I see her move to the table she

91

prefers, bringing out a notebook and pen with a secret smile I now find painfully overwritten.

I find refuge in the bar. Then I realise a khaki-clad figure has dumped her bag on the counter and may have ordered an early aperitif. It is the international photographer, no doubt reviving after an assault on the town's graphic resources. Some previous conversation has taken place between her and the young barman. I see how the photographer's unfinished stare renders the man's back tight and conscious, and how Samuel's face flinches in the mirror. This grand warren of a hotel is not without its Togolese girls and porn channels and off-duty priests. I see that the barman has been approached for some easy midday sex.

The woman delves into a large, practical-looking bag and retrieves a sachet of lens-cleaning tissues. The young barman pours her a beer. Having perused the photographer's book and now disturbed her hungry proposition-making, I feel a queer sensation of intimacy. This makes our silence seem all the more perverted.

In the evening, Margaret's presence at an ambassadorial cocktail is not essential, but merely an act of good form. I touch her shoulder in the generous suite that is our home.

'Darling, have you forgotten the Spanish cocktail this evening? I think Eric is already in the lobby.'

Margaret looks at me over a spicy ginger drink she prepares for her throat. 'I thought I'd sit it out tonight, Olivier. I haven't the strength. You know how my back gives out at those functions. I don't think I could bear to hear another frightful national day speech.'

As proof she extends herself along the settee, allowing me to study the trembling anklet I'd noticed before. I comment upon it.

'Why Olivier, it's from Nina. The woman you misunderstand. It's from the Tuareg people. You don't like it on me?'

Given its origin, the anklet appears the cheapest, gaudiest trinket.

I ignore her. 'What a pity then. I'm afraid I will have to leave you, Margaret.'

Throughout the cocktail party I feel a migraine developing behind my left eye socket. I am a tall man, and make an effort to defer the pain from my tensed facial muscles throughout my body. The ache begins to rock my concentration and needle the fibres of my neck. The Spanish Ambassador, this evening's host, is standing before me. She too has begun to enthuse about our famous guest.

'I hear you've changed the flavour of the month down your way. Quite an honour to have such an art house figure in the vicinity,' she says. Here I oscillate, unwilling to surrender my views and risk another bout of strife. We accept further drinks. The Spanish woman tells of having met Nina in a previous posting, very pleased with her story. Another dignitary speaks of an exhibition in New York. A well-respected Middle Eastern diplomat arrives and our circle widens, accolades rising into the air.

As soon as the first guests exit from beneath the sweltering canopy I salute the ring of fellow expatriates and work my way into the moist yard. A bejewelled Indian woman passes me and gives me a humoured, exquisite smile. Bothered by the heady charm of her eyes, I question my own manner. Had I approached her with stealth, with invitation? A stirring incomprehension overwhelms me. I hurry towards the car while another foreign anthem tolls through the palms.

Although I had hoped for Margaret's absence from our apartment, I feel piqued by it upon arrival. I take two of the stronger sachets from a packet we share – both lifelong migraine sufferers. My face in the mirror appears brutal. I see the tension clawing distended skin, and the wide exposed temples with their lack of erudition and hint of ruin. Neither the face of a father or husband, but an angry, ageing biped.

It is just on nine o'clock. The restaurant salon is in full swing. Businessmen on shaky contracts hunch over gravy. Nigerians sever steaks. The air crew regulars fluctuate between menu choices. I cannot see Margaret at her usual booth. Could she be in that woman's room, her gorgeous eyes entrapped in that crass lens? I recall Nina Cooke's room number, two floors below our own. The staff sense I am agitated, or are they permeated by something else? Mercy Obede glances at me from her post at the restaurant entrance and her eyes quickly divert.

I pass outdoors to the pool area. Immediately the air, pungent and humid, settles its weight upon my shoulders. I stride across the tiles to the far end of the pool. A light like a tranquil awaiting medusa sends rays through the water. Mosquitoes whine in the tossed palms. Under a canopy diners unfold menus, whilst fans whirr the thick air. Inevitably, my eyes are pulled upward over the building's façade. The emblem of the hotel chain is outlined in neon on the roof.

As I presumed, the curtains are drawn across the window of Nina Cooke's room on the fifth floor. Each suite in this hotel is identically furnished. And though the aesthetics are wan and in need of renovation, I know from the grade of the light that Nina Cooke's low bedside lamps are switched on, daubing the faded hessian curtains. I also know that my wife must be inside sharing her green-spiced eyes, their panes lured open.

The headache flares behind my eyes. I remember the practice of blood-letting, and wonder if men inflamed with ardour ever felt relief when hot trickles crept across their flesh. I also wonder if Nina Cooke has ever married, and whether she has ever carried a child as my wife has, and seen it expelled into gloved hands, creamy with vernix.

One of the waiters, a soft, secure man named Ben, approaches me. He asks should I like a light meal or one of my

94

preferred drinks. Earlier on in the year, Ben's attractive daughter fell pregnant to a French researcher staying here, who toyed with the idea of an exotic marriage. As much as I respect Ben's services and predictable character, I advised the young man to leave money with the girl, camouflage his intentions, and pursue his life plan where he belongs. Although my mixed marriage might claim otherwise, I am no herald of cultural watering-down or suffering hybrids. The French researcher vanished. Ben's daughter will eventually marry a scoundrel of her own kind. Ben looks at me, concentrating on the tones of my silence.

'No thanks, Ben. I'll take a nightcap in my room. Good evening.'

I return to the lobby. I take the empty elevator up to Nina Cooke's floor. I step out onto the carpet and look down the hall the length of the building. Several meal trays sit in front of doors, stacked with plates and half-glasses of beer. The need for food has been replaced by desire, masturbation, cable T.V. Before Nina Cooke's door I pause, in great pain, my skin damp. There is a silence I am incapable of gauging. Perhaps I hear the slight click of a camera shutter. I imagine I hear bedcovers thrown back, one or two murmurs. And yet my imagination remains sightless.

Sometime later there is a burst of alcohol or lust-induced female laughter beyond the door. I recognise Margaret's joy, released at such an exorbitant cost. I stumble down the empty hallway to the lift, almost running. The silver doors open, revealing my destroyed face on the reflective panel inside. To my left I see Mercy Obede, hands clasped, her face turned from the nudity of my emotion. As the doors cushion together she reminds me of the arrival of an eminent Nigerian writer, just off the plane from Zurich. I swear in my own tongue, sensing Margaret's estrangement is something now defined – and nearly public. Mercy bows. I find myself heaving. We resume poses of detachment before the lift discharges us downstairs.

I find the Nigerian writer altogether too brash. Patiently,

I listen to the rundown of European luminaries so reluctant to see him depart. The man amuses himself with a few anecdotes I fail to appreciate, and rather bossily suggests we have a drink. I am at the point of refusing when I see Margaret and Nina idling towards Margaret's driver Eric, now in semi-slumber by the front desk. I make out the name of a nightclub – trashy, but not the trashiest – and a message to be passed on to myself, Monsieur Olivier. The ladies depart. I find myself in a perplexed lull, obedient to the Nigerian. He sends his bags upstairs and leads me into the bar area. The pianist ripples melancholy notes above the bustle, such that one unthinkingly recalls regret.

'A fine crowd for a weeknight,' my guest says. 'And your pianist has quite a style.'

The wrenching elements of this evening have so exhausted me that the writer's tentative comments now strike a lax note. Alcohol has also subdued his post-Europe boasting. He sinks into a lounge.

'This hotel hasn't changed in decades. Most of our white elephants from the seventies are now in shambles,' he says.

'We do our best to counter the elements,' I reply.

Tasting my scotch, I can't help but plumb the reaches of my love for Margaret. It was once so vital, so tumescent. I remember the steady shards of her eyes staring upward, grown into massive orbs, the lovely delivery of her mouth.

The writer frowns at my distraction.

'It appears you have an illustrious guest in your books. Nina Cooke on her rounds again.'

'Yes,' I reply.

'Still going, that woman. She does sell well in Europe,' he says with a writer's nastiness. I am alerted.

'When my third book came out she tried it on me – the absorbing portrait business. When I saw the photos I was horrified at the way she'd put her label on me. Many have said the same of her. I've heard that when she travels in the bush she dresses everyone herself, like an American film director. She has her assistant plot every image. And mobile phones are given.'

I signal for further drinks, laughing lightly. 'Oh yes, I've heard some of that. I was shown her latest book. Quite a glamorous form of appropriation.'

The writer grins. One of his novels, I recall, stages a modern African revolution, complete with the hideous slaughter of whites.

'Correct,' he says. 'For this is the new age of bartering, the new embezzling of the spirit. Not a thing we need to celebrate,' he says, ignoring his glass.

He stands, walks over to the pianist with a weary gait. I realise his career has been lengthy and lauded, and I know next to nothing of it. He and the local pianist laugh as the notes turn to a haunting Chopin nocturne. The writer walks back and resumes his seat.

'I must apologise deeply,' he says. 'That old cultural imperialism knows no bounds.'

We pass another hour together before the pianist retires and the building's silence ushers us to bed. We shake hands in the elevator at his floor. I watch him advance down the hallway, key-card poised in hand. Throughout our conversation I have not been in a position to view Margaret's return. Mercifully, my headache has eased, though traces of it simmer as I walk the long tunnel of numbered doors to our suite. There is no sound anywhere.

I drink a scotch in our dark kitchen, ignoring the grittiness in my temples reaching down behind my eyes. In all these years I have never seethed for another woman; I have twice been tempted, but have retreated with shame. I walk into our bedroom and stand above my wife of thirty years sleeping scrolled on the sheets. Trousers, her black evening shirt, a black brassière, have all been thrown on an upholstered chair in a way that is breathless with new life. I lie behind her in my clothing and, drinking down her scent, begin to tremble as though I have a sudden fever or have been shifted to the coldest terrain. I put my cheek to her skin and feel decay winding through us.

The following morning Margaret is cheerful. Her attitude is enervating, given my heavy mood. Unusually, she has made coffee and places it on the table in a fervent way.

'Olivier, what on earth were you up to last night? Who was the extravagant guest who kept you up until all hours?'

'I should think you enjoyed a more extravagant evening overall.'

In my weariness my feelings for Margaret approach dislike. She wears a shapeless beige shirt, a pendant of manacled glass beads. I feel certain she is braless and this idea now fills me with distaste.

'You know, Olivier, I don't know why you have this attitude towards Nina. She's an artist. I've never been so surprised by you. In any case you shan't be able to redeem yourself. Nina will be heading off tomorrow. She's flying down to Jo'burg and then trekking up to Namibia.'

'And that's a cause for this inane cheerfulness?'

'Olivier,' she says, bracing against the back of her chair. 'I'm going with Nina. I've decided I have to leave. I cannot stay here any longer.' She abandons her grip on a spoon. She lifts out of her chair and moves with a type of wooden corruption.

I straighten the day-old newspaper.

'I have an appointment with Nina,' she says, and exits.

I stare down at the newspaper and my eyes snag upon an article about a doomed convoy of Scandinavians who have been taken hostage by a group of Tuaregs, the men Nina Cooke photographs with their dark eye-liner and indigo cloth. There is a stock image of tribesmen with their expensive guns and rusty vehicles. Below there is a chequer-board photograph of the missing Scandinavians. I read their intricate names and look into their balanced smiles and enchanted, gleaming eyes.

YOUNG BRITISH MAN DROWNS IN ALPINE LAKE

Tom's father frowns at Corinne again. This is the moment I expect to scroll down and see into her face, a clear and unwritten page. I want her to provide this.

But Corinne's eyes close and her lips grow thin. Another spasm passes Tom's father's features and I see there is a primal animal in there. He wants to raise his builder's hands to Corinne's neck.

Tom's father wants to know why, in the middle of January, his fiercely intelligent son dropped his jeans and went skinny-dipping in a mountain lake.

He nears Corinne's face one more time. He is gleaning it for ashen traces. Of which there are, for one who knows her. He cannot see how the colour of her lips has dropped a shade towards the blue end of red, a drop in blood pressure as much as a realignment of pluck, and that her huge white forehead, template for her sticky righteousness, lies galvanised beneath its compelling shirr. They say the hydraulics of the face are spellbinding. Corinne's face is giving him so much information I am appalled.

Corinne's face now pulls apart. The unwritten page is provided. Corinne crumples and begins to cry.

I take her into my arms again, kissing her temples where I imagine the blood in its wiring runs close to the surface. She feels so cold. Tom's father backs off, swearing at us.

Tom passed away in the ambulance, somewhere between Lago Santa Croce and the hospital in Belluno. That's what I was told. Amazingly, he was still alive when they pulled him out, the resilience Tom displayed in abseiling and wintry sailing put to its final test. We followed the ambulance which took off at a crazy speed, but lost track of it quickly. We took the wrong carriageway on the *autostrada* and ended up in Vittorio Veneto, then wound back to Belluno on a state road, sliding on day-old snow. We simply got lost, had to ask directions to the hospital, the slowly resounding obscenity of what had happened dove-tailing with the very banality that was taking place.

Tom's girlfriend Mary sees dots on the mountain flank. We work out they are skiers heading downward in tight S-curves – the ultimate motion – along a lush blue pleat in the snow. The mountain is colossal. Some sort of palpable convection pulverises your thought and sucks you inward, spits you out. I enjoy being so small. We look carefully and see there are still more dots making their ascent. They are climbing vertically towards a sling of whiteness between one outcrop and the first shoulders of the peak. The biggest slide in the park. They can't make it. They won't. In twenty minutes and two more espressos to the unnecessary beat of Jamiroquai, they have.

The girls drink coffee, losing interest in the skiers, maintaining their guise of getting along. It's not working, the Mary-and-Corinne thing. It's far from the first time our unmatched girlfriends don't hook up. Tom seems tired and I know he'd rather conserve his best energy for the snow, not Mary's delights on a narrow bunk. Thankfully Corinne's seasoned stubbornness is more pliant. I watch her eyes drift over the peaks then back to her nails, to the grain of the wood, to a declaration of love some teenager has carved there. For a second, I think of eating raw fish. It must be the purity of the elements: the zinging air, the grey seamed wood, Corinne's flesh.

Tom watches the skiers trace their compass-set arcs. In my head I try to project myself up there too, away from the bar and the bright sports clothing, the bombastic nature of every Italian conversation now accessorised by the full-volume Supertramp song some retro has fished out. The silent combustion of the mountain caught in its geological yaw. The

100

taut air pulsing in your throat in burning breaths. Breaking the pearly crust with an easy *plush-plush-plush*.

But Tom and I are crap on the snow, and boarders anyway. Right now no dream feels more elusive.

'Let's do a run,' Tom says.

We strap our front bindings over our broad boots, easing in the serrated tongue towards its comfortable *click*. Tom waves a gloved hand to the girls as he paddles off to the top of the slope, collapsing to the ground again as he fits in his rear foot. I don't see if the girls respond. My eyes are still on the last skier of the group, his final slices leaving a graffiti squiggle before he disappears below the tree line. Tomorrow morning the massive mountain will have erased all traces of his path.

I reach the spot where Tom had been fastening up and catch sight of him already at the base of the first part of the slope, arms splayed and knees braced as he finishes his last curve. Irritated that I have to chase him, I bumble on downward. I am no athlete and Tom has spent almost two decades reminding me my efforts are exclusively valiant, entirely deprived of both talent and skill. I reach him, out of breath, as he shuttles off for a series of swift curves close to the edge of the slope, out of the radius of a couple of beginner skiers. His pelvis engineers the back and forward tilting of the board as he picks up speed, his extended arms keeping his upper body balanced and on course. He looks back towards me, he wants to see me watching. I wave. Then I see what Tom has not yet seen. A snowmobile jetting up his side of the slope, about to accelerate over a bump that obscures Tom's vision. Two locals with sharp eyes and broom moustaches sit braced together, now connected to the crescendo of a motor's buzz.

But Tom turns away in time and up-thrust fingers are exchanged by both parties. Tom heads back to the middle of the slope. Burnt two-stroke fuel dissolves on the air.

I reach him at the lift. He's been watching me on the last

part and is keen to give me tips rather than harp on about the near-miss. Much of Tom's professional success lies in his technical exactness, though it means he has a string of Marys wheedling in the night. We do several more slopes. By the third, Tom's tips begin to pay off and on the easiest incline I feel both the board and my feet strapped to it are becoming marginally more obedient. The board cuts from side to side and my spine stays in place, as I ease my pelvis and thighs onto the list of the curve. Inside my boots my toes are clenched so hard I can't tell whether they are hot or cold. Sweat soaks my buttocks and back.

Then I stop. My goggles are I fogged. I unzip pockets hoping I brought some of Corinne's tissues. The slope is empty but I'm so happy with my progress I don't care if Tom is a mile further down. A greyness has lowered onto the world. *Snow.* The first flakes trickle down uncertainly, a slow shower apparent against the wet green of the trees. But it is too warm for the snow to stick yet. I put out my tongue to feel the same needles I did as a child.

I find Tom at the bar halfway down the slope rearranging his jacket and gloves on a heater built like tiled ceramic box. He has ordered a beer and is trying his Italian on the bored waitress with curly long hair and tarty green eye-shadow. I recall that the slopes empty quickly when it snows. The car park below will be choked with revving vehicles and city people on their knees trying to put on snow chains. I wonder if the girls have moved inside close to the fireplace: Surely Corinne must have delineated a field fit for conversation.

Tom and I drink three or four beers each and take turns going out the back to piss. The waitress has a name now – Ambra – meaning amber, as in the resin that is sometimes flecked with prehistoric gnats. I've come close enough now to see her challenging nose piercing and quite big teeth, and how Tom has taken an unyielding shine to her. I see he wants her, in the way he often wants a woman when he has one at hand. Over the years there have been women he hungers for and takes home to bed, only to – I sense – leave them hurting in the dark. For a woman Tom's body is probably too powerful.

Apparently Ambra's brother was one of the skiers who freestyle-skied down the mountain today. Ambra asks if we saw them earlier, putting an endearing effort into her precise English. Tom is stoked by both factors. Ambra's desirability climbs. I don't even ask Tom if we should hunt down our own girlfriends. My phone has no reception in this depression at the bottom of the run and the snow is gathering along the window panes. I walk over and take a look outside. The snowflakes are as big as small fists. A few more skiers come onto the terrace, stomping caked boots and shaking off white shoulder-pads. They enter. They are pallid with broad bony faces and might be from Slovenia. Ambra prepares them a tray of mulled wine and slides back to Tom. He asks questions about her brother, who is close to Tom's age it seems, who instructs with one of the ski schools. She says he goes up when conditions are good, which wasn't entirely the case today, describing these in meteorological terms which are music to Tom's ears.

I found Corinne weeping on the boot of my car after a hard night in the city. Mine is a dull area and finding a beautiful sobbing French woman in the night was akin to finding a real fairy at the bottom of the garden. I couldn't get it out of her, what had happened, whether she'd been gang-raped by punks or her cat had been flattened by a car. Despite being in incredibly bad shape and having an early start the next day, I urged her into the house, made some strong tea and set her up on the couch. As I took my last look at her wilted eyes and pale forehead settling under the emergency duvet, she beckoned me.

I made ruthless love to her, the fact that I had no claim to her meant I sought no democracy and nothing divine. The stuff I'd smoked made me draw into her and imagine I was

103

expanding and could stay inside her for hours. But she wanted it. She hovered on the brim for a long time. A strange thing, she cooperated, and occasionally smiled, though I looked away from her. She was fit, fitter than I was, and you could tell she loved her own body and inhabited every organ, every crinkle of it.

Afterwards I left her, cleaned myself, and she turned to the wall.

Tom never believed in the Corinne-and-Markus thing. He made jokes about the fat Brit and the smashing Parisian. *She's sleeping around, you can be sure of it,* he would say. *Don't think you could ever be enough. I've seen it in her.*

Early on, Corinne told me she was abused as a child. We were sitting on Ikea stools in Tom's kitchen in the dregs of the night. I thought it was a poor line – who hadn't had an uncle's palm skate across their balls? Her mother had had a string of oversexed boyfriends who all laid their hands over her. It turned me on, the dirtiness. I liked it when she didn't wash and, at a party, she pretended she had no interest in me.

I told Tom she was the woman I would take to the grave.

Ten months later she disappeared back to Paris, claiming her mother was ill. She telephoned me in strange whispers or in a halting hoarse voice. It took longer than I wished to let her go. I'd wake up feeling her feet rubbing mine, or my soft cock nursed by the crook of her arse while she half-snored. Never had I relished the articulation of my working days with such bliss, book-ended as they were by her dreamy *séjours* at the house.

Tom took me under his wing after she left, buffering me from myself. We turned thirty-four the same week and drove up to Edinburgh. Blind drunk most of the time, we made an effort to go to some Fringe shows and round up some female attention. Tom reeled in a dancing understudy called Jody and was set. I knocked about with a student called Erin until her weird body smell overcame me and I kicked out her out one night after midnight, man down and full of shame, went to the bathroom

104

and puked.

Tom swaggers over with another frothy beer. It appears Ambra's concentration has lapsed and the beer is half head, half amber nectar. A metaphor for Tom's current condition. He leaves me at the encrusted window and goes back to the girl with green-hooded eyes and a washer from a tool-box threaded through her nose. I imagine them at it – it isn't hard – Tom thrusting into her as he would thrust over the mountain past the skiers he wishes he could impress. I sit down. The other skiers are speaking in Slovenian, I am almost certain, probably about their return to their hotel. They look doubtfully outside. Their eyes fall upon the glazed pine tabletop and they call Ambra for fresh drinks, grappa this time. Ambra comes out from behind the counter in low jeans with firm flesh showing below her T-shirt. She has a small waist and an ample bosom hiked up firmly, she must have to shop well to keep them in place.

As she returns to the counter she strikes a pose next to Tom, who knows her body is on show for him. He manages to stroke her side, she touches his forearm. I lay my head back and it hits a hard pine curlicue.

I see shapes outside. They become tall men shaking off jackets. They thud into the room bringing a wave of wetness and a dense clean smell. Everyone turns to them. Already I know they are the skiers we saw on the mountain this morning. How many were there? Five? Six? Or seven? I drink my foamy beer and watch Tom trying to read them, already placing himself in competition. Ambra shouts out to them in dialect and Tom is thrown off-balance. He tightens up, straightening his shoulders.

The group of men order a variety of drinks. Hot milk, beer, a hot tea, some grappa. I can understand that much. They are like members of an elongated race. Even Ambra looks misshapen next to them and I can feel Tom's insecurity pushing, unfurling. I have known him long enough to know how callously he feels these confrontations. Ambra points to him and the tall men suddenly notice him holding up the bar. He puts out a sheepish palm. They extend hands, their group softens. Ambra chatters with all of them, her eyes open wider and her gestures are those of a busy sister, a busy future wife. Tom notices this. Gone is the seductive touching and slowness. She has him meet her brother, a carbon copy without the eye-shadow and vulgar piercing, a giant man with her round face, the same face Tom has been thinking of pushing between his legs for the past hour and a half. Ambra's brother is shy, he teaches foreigners to ski all day, speaking English still embarrasses him. His sister doesn't seem to notice and sends Tom over another drink gaily.

Tom brings himself over to me and sits down. He begins peering out the window at the heavy woollen clots. I can't see anything now – the fold of the slope, the triangle of trees, the braid of pylons and lift seats. I have a comfortable entrapped feeling, as though I don't care if the snow presses us into the earth like a capsule with pine curlicues and faded geraniums and stuffed falcons on the wall.

Tom stands up and removes his gloves from the heater. The Slovenians glance at him. I know Tom feels they have witnessed everything. The girl with the big knockers has gone back to her brethren. The silly English are drinking beer alone. If the warmth and alcohol hadn't already burnished our features, Tom would be blushing. Tom walks over and settles our bill. There is a catch between Ambra's green-hooded eyes.

'You go outside? Now?' The ring of mountain brethren turns across to frown. 'You must be joke! Stay and drink, no?'

Tom just grins at her, salutes the Slovenians and the tall skiers, cocks his head and expects me to spring into place.

'In this? Are you mad? I'm not going out in that,' I say to him. 'Let's have a grappa and wait for it to pass.'

'I'm not staying here any longer,' Tom replies. 'We're nearly at the end of the slope. You can stay here and have a grappa if you like. Make your own way down later and I'll see you at the hotel.'

Tom's eyes leave off from mine. This is why women take such a long time to leave him. Tom *does* take off and they *do* make their own way down in the dark, craving his unsparing logic. I figure poor Mary is down to her last rations of humiliation and resolve.

I swear under my breath, picking up my gloves as a jostle of mirth travels around the group of tall skiers. They have seen idiotic foreigners before, crossing their mountains. I would have liked to have made a minor appeal on Tom's behalf. *Believe me, he's a great chap, he's a competitive bastard but it all pans out. He's come from nothing you see, has his father's massive chip on his shoulder.*

Only it would have sounded naff. Still, standing just behind him as he opens the stained pine door and an eddy of snowflakes pushes in, I feel I am on Tom's side against the world. I also feel an inkling of being physically dissolved and this startles me.

Our boards are buried under inches of snow and we are drunk. I try to ignore this fact as I ram my boot into the binding and miss, and the edge slices up and over the top of my knuckles. I look at the exposed epidermis filling with blood and let a couple of drops fall into the snow. Tom is up, both feet in and flippering about like a penguin. I pull my foot on course, jimmy in the binding tongue, and fix the rear one too. I put my goggles on but they are full of snow and useless. We should have helmets but one of our bags was lost on the flight and Tom refused to fork out for trendy Italian equipment.

'Which way?' I call out. More than anything, I want to slow Tom down before he takes off like a bat out of hell, whether or not his audience can see him.

'Over here!' I hear Tom shout, but already he is covered in blobs. The quiet, the heaviness, suddenly feel asphyxiating. I can't remember if this is a blue or a red slope, whether we have done it before even. But we have, I suddenly remember we've done it every day we've been here. With the girls before and after us, Corinne an agile experienced skier and Mary with her determined snowploughs, well-chosen accompanists for our middling curves. How different it had been yesterday! Now I can hardly see the ridge of trees and Tom's body looks like a yeti on a dying screen.

'Tom! Thomas! Wait!'

I wonder if Tom is as drunk and blinded as I am, or if he is thriving on the apparition of the real mountain men, challenging them in a rush of endorphins riding the beer. But he'll get down there, it's a given. I am bumping through wedges and pillows of snowdrift, the goggles on my forehead providing a brief shield from the driven flakes. I think I am going downward, but then the board slows and the ground is flat. I make out a tree, then a bank of them, each one fattened with white carousel arms. I read a bestseller about climbers dying like flies on Everest. The ferocious white-out and the trail of half-blackened bodies, each one propped against the ice in a mauled stupor. My anger bursts through: *Tom has no right to do this.*

Then I think logically. I remember watching Corinne's tight pants whizzing over this last section of the slope yesterday, entranced by her perfection, proud of it. Corinne, who has a French woman's adherence to rules if only to upend them, will be angry we have taken off in such idiotic conditions. She has an unpredictable tolerance for Tom's enterprises.

I hear a quick whistling sound behind the whiteness. It is not Tom. Two of the skiers materialise, one of them is Ambra's expert brother. Tom is not going to like this. The word *rescue* will kill him. But perhaps he is already at the bottom, taking a leak, pissed off that he has let Ambra slip away.

'*Stai bene? Vuoi seguirci giù?*'

Whatever they said, I nod hard. I assume it wasn't *Hey,*

we've come for your girlfriend. They stand there in lax positions, leaning on their ski stocks for support, the snow falling on their faces.

Tom's father is staying at a little hotel close to the slopes. He wanted it that way, not near the lake or the hospital, God forbid. He wanted a couple of days here before he flew out. Mary organised everything. Mary has evolved from the girlfriend Tom was preparing to cast off to a tear-streaked organiser. I guess she still has a store of resolve left, haunting her probably. Tom's father smokes in the small hotel car park in the sharp sunlight, watching families pack their gear and have their squabbles before leaving for the slopes. He takes everybody in, eating them with his northern English eyes. Everyone knows about the tragedy. Mary sweeps up to him. She cries into his big chest and dwindles within his massive arms. Tom was so wiry, a spare man whose physical strengths were technical and acquired. I'm sure the old man beat him.

I wonder if – for Mary – they have a whiff of the same scent.

Corinne and I begin to pack. Corinne won't face Tom's father again. She lies in bed. This morning she went for a walk in the woods and I was certain I would come across her body curled under a snowy tree, the same way Tom's had been folded on the ground and gently covered, already so lifeless.

From our balcony I can see the end of the slope Tom led me onto the other afternoon when it was snowing. Ambra's slope, I now call it. Today the sky is brilliant and the snow is still hooked on the trees. Tom would have been up in the fresh powder, paddling off-piste, telling me what a tosser I am and how Mary liked it up her backside. I turn back to Corinne. She is asleep.

The lake stretches out black like a maw in the side of the

earth. Yesterday's snow covers the surrounding mountains in shocking violet moonlight. A high altitude discotheque. The disco ball a galactic spray. We were lucky the local snowploughs were so deft and Ambra's directions proved decipherable and correct. This looks like the right place. A tiny wooden bar with a stage next to it. Big speakers. Chrome microphone stands. Laid-back groupies chugging beers. The shock of a bass riff in the thick of the woods, so impertinent.

Tom parks the car in the cleared area. Other cars are streaming down the hill. An older guy puts on a fluorescent traffic jacket and begins to line up the arriving cars. Tom looks about. Corinne and I wander over to the bar to watch the band setting up. Behind the zone of light the land descends steeply into the inky water, trees braking along the edge. There are no boats or jetties in sight here, no relic of any other season than this.

There is a pause in the clinking of bottles and talk. A sound that is complete nothingness expands, until a car in descent sloshes over it.

Mary hasn't come with us. I suppose Tom allowed a tussle to brew in order to free himself for Ambra, but he'll tell me afterwards. Corinne and I order beers. She doesn't care either way. She is tired of Tom and I pushing down the slopes on our adult learning curves. She mastered skiing decades ago. She thinks we are stupid.

I spot one of the Slovenians who had been at the snow-covered bar yesterday. I am surprised when he waves to me. Am I so visible? I wave back. I take it as a sure sign that Ambra will turn up and Tom will get his home run. The band starts up suddenly. It is an old Clash song, sung in strangled English words learnt in a mountain classroom. I can't help thinking that it is admirable, the head-banging becoming grammatical research. The music rises in a restless bubble.

I look at Corinne and she rolls her eyes.

Tom appears. It seems Ambra hasn't turned up yet. But

who knows what hamlet she hails from, how many round-faced brothers she has to cook for, and the potency of her car. Tom nods with the music and holds his beer bottle by the neck. He is wearing a cashmere grey scarf over his striped boarding jacket, urban-meets-mountain, to be lost on the girl with the clunky nose-ring. I touch the small of Corinne's back. She turns around to me and I see how she was in the hotel room when I arrived yesterday. In soapy bath water up to her neck, face reddened, hair wet, watching me peel away the shrouds of my clothes.

She whispers something to me but I don't hear well, the music has morphed into some Bowie song but I can't remember which. She loves Bowie, I don't. Perhaps she wants to dance. She drags Tom away. I watch the illogical pair they make, printed one over the other, zigzagging through the crowd.

The music changes to the worst rendition I have ever heard of *Purple Haze*. I realise this is just short of insanity, standing on a strip of sodden earth between the creaking templates of mountain and lake, listening to ruptured Hendrix. I am so cold my body smells pungent, as though the sweat is stoppered in my pores. And there is another smell I can't identify, lifting on the air. Like overturned earth, or the entrails of water. I look above the nodding heads to the carapace of blackness. It is the inverse of yesterday's comforting burial by snow. It is the harshest territory I have ever seen.

CLAUDIA CARDINALE'S FLESH-COLOURED LIPS

Marina came in when he was eating grapes in front of an old Claudia Cardinale film. Unannounced, since last weekend had ended in a cloud of mutual, unrepenting bad will. Sebastien Tempels wanted to hear how she would get around it.

'Her breasts look like a pair of Tupperware containers,' she said as she tossed her bag.

She sat down, taking a sprig of his grapes, staring at the delicate scene of love that he had been waiting for. A glance told him she had been plotting these moments all week. On the screen, Claudia Cardinale's flesh-coloured lips locked with those of her partner.

'Hello, Sebastien.'

He went into the kitchen without speaking. During the week he had gone through vulnerable moods. On a dreadful day he had invited another girl back to his place. She had lain out on the kitchen bench, strumming herself and laughing.

Now tell me if this isn't something you've seen in a second-rate movie, she had said.

It was, he had told her. He'd told her to get down.

He took out a cup and switched on the kettle. The evening light drifted down from a rooftop window onto the lids of things. He took out a second cup resignedly, and the cheap brand of tea he knew would keep him awake for the next few hours. He took a swig of vodka to compensate for it.

That week he had failed a fairly important exam. In essence, it had been about the composition of blood. Sebastien hadn't been able to access the knowledge he knew his brain was holding from him. He'd accused Marina of pillaging his concentration, but he knew it was his brain that had slammed shut.

He held his mug and thought about the other girl, the one who'd lain back on the kitchen bench the night he'd failed the exam. She followed his course at the university. She was tricky: she slept with one of the female lecturers, it was rumoured, although he hadn't had the nerve to ask if it were true. The girl was called Caroline. Sebastien, until the moment on the bench, had thought he desired her. When he had told her to get down she'd had a torn look and had asked for a glass of milk.

Sebastien came back out into the low-ceilinged room with the two cups of tea and fairly good intentions. But it was empty and the television was blank.

A year later Marina was hit by a car as she crossed Chausée de Vleurgat at night. She was taken to a nearby hospital to be treated for a deep cut on her chin, where she had received the impact of her fall. She had no other injury apart from bruised, jarred limbs which would pain her for a full week afterwards. She called her father who lived back in Devon and told him that she would be kept under observation in hospital for twenty-four hours. She begged him not to come.

At this stage in her life Marina was alone. She had tried to paint after following a course and for six months or so she had heard herself say she was a painter to people she met for the first time. The thought of this now stung her. Since she had left Sebastien she had applied for a job as a translator and been unsuccessful. Her father was supporting her and she was collecting unemployment benefits from home.

She woke up the first morning after her accident with Sebastien's face forming in front of hers. A shiver travelled over her body and her vision blurred with tears. She felt a rush of everything she had failed to experience that year, culminate.

When she was released from hospital their story resumed. Their bodies fell into a duel ease that coincidence had blessed.

Marina came to sleep at Sebastien's each Friday, Saturday and Sunday nights. During the week he worked long, odd hours and told her he didn't like the idea of someone waiting for him. He earned little money, and what he could spare he was saving for a holiday in Argentina. As far as he was concerned, the question of money hadn't been resolved between them. Sebastien felt that Marina could have cooked a little, or offered to replace some of the bottles of vodka she guzzled regularly. For when Marina was with him all she could do was admire him from a stool in the kitchen, make cosmetic rearrangements of his possessions, and wait as he did for their inevitable collapse into sex.

'Oh, this is such a cute little vase! Did you get it at the markets? If you had a pair of them you could put them on the mantelpiece and look entirely Art Deco. Is it Art Deco?'

Sebastien never told Marina about Caroline, the woman he had nearly slept with when he was a student. For him Caroline had provided a small flare when his study was at a critical nexus. He had kicked himself for months afterwards, and gradually he had forgotten the reason why they had never had sex. Then one morning in October, Caroline rang the buzzer downstairs when he was having a second round of coffee. That night in casualty an old, unclaimed woman had grasped him before the life fled out of her. Sebastien's hands still carried the chill.

They embraced at the door. He brought her into the kitchen and for a time they talked easily.

'Tell me, Sebastien, last year, why is it that you didn't want to sleep with me? Why did you back down?'

Sebastien flushed. He'd forgotten the sensation and momentarily followed the flaring capillaries along his skin. The explosion.

'There was someone else. I'm back with her, actually.'

'You know that doesn't count. You knew I had it, didn't you? You suspected it.'

'Had what?'

'The plague, you fool. I've got the damned plague and you'd have it too if you'd been with me.'

He watched her break down. He expected the encounter was the idea of some therapist helping her come to terms with the disease. She left after they had talked about hospitals and where the best treatment was available in Brussels. Sebastien never saw her again.

Later, in traffic, he thought of that night when she had hoisted herself up onto the kitchen bench and smoothly lain back. He had wanted her until then. He had wanted her until she had said something about a second-rate film. If she hadn't said whatever she had said he knew he would have bonked her, easily. But he hadn't.

Thereafter, every time Sebastien entered Marina the shock of this potential collision acted as a charge. It became a part of him, scar tissue webbed on his nerves. The thought that he had not had Caroline Moreau was a sickening impulse he continued to feel first hand. With time, even after he learned that Caroline had been buried in Metz, this feeling neither softened nor went away.

OPAQUE

Theirs was a good marriage, it worked. After the children the sex had been forced, even rudimentary, until something sweeping had happened and they fell undivided into the same current. But very early one morning her husband Yaw went to the front gates where she heard Henry Osei's massive Land Rover revving. Yaw came back leading Henry's fair-skinned three-year-old through the house.

'What on earth is going on?' She pulled a cloth around her naked body. The child wasn't hers; as a kid she'd hated naked adults.

Yaw was crouched to the small boy with his cropped soft curls, the same curls their kids had but looser on the scalp. The boy looked enquiring, half-awake.

'We're just looking after him for a few days while Henry and Frances sort things out.'

'What do you mean? Does Frances know Henry's brought him here?' She felt a cold thumping in her gut. Yaw had crossed borders before; at the back of their shoe cupboard Yaw had a gun.

Yaw looked at her. 'Nobody has to know he's here. Tell the house-girls the mother has gone back to Europe. On holidays. Or to see her family.'

She stared at her husband. Henry Osei had startled everybody when he'd picked up Frances Connelly. The love had been hot and quick but had turned fast. Frances had other children with the man she'd left for Henry Osei. She'd seen them at the international school. They were shell-shocked and feeble-looking, children who ran recklessly under the sun. She looked at their half-brother in her kitchen, and her husband's large hand on the child's small shoulder. The boy wore a checked shirt, a hand-me-down from a big brother, and a too-big pair of sandals.

'Here, take him. I think he needs a clean.'

She heard her own children rousing upstairs. Philippa and Julius would soon be down for cereal and cartoons. 'I can't do this Yaw. This is wrong.'

'Nothing is wrong, Marika,' Yaw said, fixing her. '*Nothing*. If Frances knew how to behave this wouldn't have to happen. Trust me, Henry will sort her out. Now do as I say, will you?'

She walked over and held out her hand to the boy. She called his name. As she pronounced it she felt the sweat prickle in her armpits. He turned to her and she tugged him along the hallway to the bathroom.

The child was indeed dirty and seemed strained when she changed his nappy. He was a little old for nappies, but she supposed Frances had her hands full. He also had a touch of the runs and his faeces were dark and poisonous. She taped one of Julius' night-time nappies on him and was glad her children had come downstairs. Soon the tears would start, she knew. It would be better to get him fed up and sat in front of the T.V.

She went upstairs when the children were settled and the morning nanny had arrived to supervise. Yaw had showered and was dressing to leave for work.

'What do I do with him? How long is this going to last? What if Frances calls the house?'

'No one will call. Henry will pass tonight and probably this will all be over.'

Yaw tucked a printed shirt into jeans, then pulled it out in front of the mirror. It was a friend's design and she didn't much like it.

'How does this look? Tucked in or out?'

'I don't know, Yaw. Decide for yourself.' She walked into their bathroom, threw off her cloth and sat down naked to pee. As she urinated she wondered why the boy had never cried as she changed him. Why he had so willingly consigned himself to them in their kitchen. It must have been his way. Some children were like that. They accepted everything, their eyes were the darkest pools.

Yaw came into the bathroom and watched her quickly wipe herself. 'I'll be gone all day. Just keep a lid on this and everything will be fine.'

She heard Yaw's old Peugeot moving up the street and visualised him shuffling his balls, peering over neighbours' glass-cropped fences, waving at the mammies on the corner. They all knew Henry was a loose cannon, and that Frances was a British woman who'd been flirting with him at the pub. They'd all thought it had been a game at first, the usual plucking out of a local by the golden hand, a spate of blessed shagging. But then Frances Connelly had rolled up to Ryan's with a five-month belly – even Marika had been shocked – by which time the minor diplomat husband had been shelved and the lovers left a rocking wake wherever they went beaming.

They'd given birth weeks apart in the same clinic, Frances with her love-child, Marika with little Julius. But they never met in those early months, until a year or so later when Henry's timber interests had tied him to one of Yaw's building projects. Then Frances had come a few times to Marika's house with Henry, where she expelled her older white kids like a gawky sun-struck litter into the yard. The children were rough, they played as if in a trance, speaking to each other in rare swift sentences. Frances ignored them, keen to keep the mercurial Henry in sight. Between them there was a tangible oscillation, though many of Frances' comments felt staged, expressed with awkward guilt, as though even she knew she shouldn't be there.

Then their lives carried on when Henry and Yaw had their usual falling out. Friends from childhood, the men were quick to mend this. Only Frances took it to heart with the coldness of a woman who has injured, and Marika hardly ever spoke to her again.

Marika turned on the shower and stood under the broad fitting Yaw had brought back from Dubai. She turned the lateral jets onto her thighs and felt the skin needled with little spears. Then she turned it off, standing there, her skin buzzing, listening to the pitch of the house. She heard nothing. With Yaw there had been dozens of crazy projects and massive head-rolling failure but he was always able to withdraw and regroup; each time he came back with a fresh business partner and a new enthralled momentum.

Now she felt a deep churning in her gut. What had Frances Connelly done that they had to punish her like this? Henry would never tell her, or he would in distracted, mumbled words. She heard her daughter talking bossily downstairs. She touched herself. If they had had sex before he left she would have felt calmer about this, less visual. She could see Frances Connelly in twisted bed sheets, staring at the wall.

Angela called. She was grateful Angela hadn't clicked through the house in her kitten heels and the slim, tea-stained legs she was so proud of. That they were harbouring Frances Connelly's child, it was now palpable, criminal even.

'Marika? Is that you?'

'Of course it's me.'

'Is anyone on the other line?'

'No, there is not. Why should there be?'

'I just saw Henry in traffic at Danquah Circle.'

'And?'

She and Angela had been sent off to boarding school together as scared, big-eyed girls, and had come back with cornrows and refined degrees to find husbands. But Angela was childless.

'Nothing. He was headed off to the site, I suppose. How are the kids?'

'They're fine. Philippa's better but I don't think I'll send her to nursery today.'

She had a ghastly thought: What if her five-year-old talked? What if she was quizzed and the words came out? *Yes, he's playing at our house. He came over all day to play.* Coercing Philippa, telling her not to talk, burning these things in her mind like bleach on the skin.

'Apparently Henry Osei and Frances Connelly had an enormous bust-up. She was going to take the kids back to England. Even the little one.'

'Oh.'

'I never disliked Frances, you know. People should have given her a chance.'

'Angie, I have stuff to do this morning.'

'Yesterday I was coming home from the Institute, not too late, before six I think, along Ring Road. I had a taxi in front, full of white kids in the back seat, then I noticed Henry Osei's Land Rover ahead, slowing down to make a U-turn back to the beach. A white woman got out of the taxi and started running after him, hurtling herself down the highway in the traffic. She was trying to get a look inside the jeep. Henry drove off and she just kept running after him. Until he was too fast and she had to stop. It was Frances Connelly.'

'Are you sure it was her?'

'And the worst was that it was her older kids in the taxi, they were all pressed to the window watching their mother running down the road, and Henry driving off. It was truly awful.'

'Have you any idea why?' Marika's voice nearly cracked.

'Later, Paul told me Henry called him. Said he and Frances were having problems. That she wanted to take his son back to the U.K. and he was terrified of never seeing the kid again. He asked Paul if we would take him for a few days. You know, hide him from Frances. Paul was furious. You know Paul.'

'Yes.'

'Apparently he's roving about with this child, getting help from the family to hide him. It's wrong, it's just sickening. What if that woman goes to her embassy? Or the police?'

Marika's insides hollowed. But the woman's embassy would be slow to help one who had so brazenly turned from the fold. Likewise, the police would think she was a sex-stricken woman served her just desserts. She heard a strange tearless cry from downstairs. It was Henry's child in the kitchen.

'Angela, I think they need me downstairs. Be a doll and let me go to them.' Angela didn't seem to notice how quiet her voice was, how impaired. 'We'll talk afterwards.'

'Oh, go and masturbate. I could tell Yaw didn't deliver this morning.'

She pushed away the phone and clutched her cloth to her front. She had to call Yaw. Yaw *knew*, and he had counted on her complicity. She had provided him this the moment she took the child's hand in the kitchen and felt the sweat welling under her arms, prickling, making curlicues on her skin as she led him to the bathroom and hoisted his light body onto the changing table, as she squirted cleaning gel onto a ball of cotton wool and eased the putrid fibres away from his skin. She had cleaned his tiny genitals as a profound treachery snagged in her belly.

She let the cloth drop, sitting cross-legged on the bed. She knew she had Frances Connelly's phone number saved on her phone, and that somewhere Frances would be ready to snatch hers to her cheek, praying for intervention.

But if she called she would perforate all that she held close to her. It would cost her her life.

Again, she heard the child's dry moaning. She pulled on a pair of jeans and a tight ribbed T-shirt. She would go out and buy the kids water pistols and have them play in the yard. When Henry Osei came around tonight she would hand the child over and give Henry a piece of her mind. Then, later, she would straddle her husband and he would steer into her and they would clasp in love. She headed down the stairs to try to comfort Frances Connelly's boy. She was good with children.

MONTGOMERY AKUOFO, FATHER OF TWINS

The way that Faustina told him, it was wrong. He was sitting at an empty chop bar on the roadside, waiting for the French woman's green car to pass. He took out the mobile phone she had bought for him and it was Faustina, who told him she was expecting twins, his twins. *They are two boys!* she said with much enthusiasm. Twins had not visited their village for an age. He folded the phone shut and put it in his pocket. The French woman drove past and he saw her son was not in the car. That was as good a sign as any. Some moments later he strode up to her gate.

By the time he reached her flat the woman had opened the door onto the rooftop and unbottled the hot air in the rooms. He could feel the air shifting about, its heat dusting his skin before it made its escape. He heard her in the shower. He stripped off his shirt and ate a banana in the kitchen. Then he opened a cold beer from her fridge, sitting on her kitchen chair, his spirits mixed. He had stolen from her, just once. It was a photograph of her family which was sitting on the bookshelf. The daughter in Europe when she was a small girl, the hard-faced son a baby on her hip. She had asked him for it and he had lied. He had kept the photo for a while then thrown it in the gutter.

'Montgomery, you're here.' She glanced at him sitting there, her eyes moving off his body. 'I should have called you. Miguel is on his way home with a friend. They stayed after school for a football match. I cannot see you now.'

His hands hung either side of the chair. He felt his cock beginning to thicken in his jeans.

'Look, you'd better get dressed. Don't be angry with me. You know there'll be other times.'

Outside, yards below them, the iron gate was cranked

open and she frowned. He pulled on his shirt. On his way downstairs he passed a pair of giggling white ten-year-olds.

He walked back to Kojo's house. He was glad he had drunk the beer. He thought of her speaking to the children in her language, sending them downstairs to play with the neighbourhood kids, something the whites did rarely. He couldn't understand why she didn't have a man of her own and he had asked her and she had tried to explain it to him. *I loved a man very much, but he didn't want to live with me. I loved another and he used to hit me hard.* When she whimpered he had held her, stroked her, trying to imagine these men's faces.

Kojo was leaving for the hospital to bring food for his brother and was soon gone. Montgomery sat down, pulled out his phone. There were no calls. The French woman put credit money in his phone but she did not give him cash. Just once, she had paid his bus fare back to the village. He called her.

'*Allô?*'

'This is Montgomery.'

'Er, hello. Is there anything wrong?'

'Come and meet me for a drink.'

'You know I can't. Not tonight.'

'My girlfriend is pregnant. The girl from the village. She is having twins.'

'Oh, Montgomery! That's quite a piece of news. Are you upset? I hope she is well. I, er, don't know what to say to you. I have to go now. I'm really sorry, try to understand.'

'I love you, Mona.'

'Yes, Montgomery. Yes.'

He was hungry. He had shown her where they grilled tilapia and served it with *banku*. He had shown her where they served *atcheke* from Ivory Coast. He had taken her to Circle at night and made her bump next to him on the dance floor. They had eaten at Honest Chef afterwards and she moved his hand between her legs in the taxi all the way home. If she were younger, he would give her a baby.

He left Kojo's and began to walk towards Rawlings Park. He would get there after nightfall. There his old aunt would feed him.

Faustina called him again in the morning.

'Monty Monty Monty! Oh, my Montgomery! How is your work?' she asked him.

He knew she was sitting in a booth in the tiny communication centre in the sun, sweat down her back, her wide eyes far apart. Faustina was an easy woman to have, she opened wide and her passage clasped him, pulling him hard. Then she pushed him off, her hair sticking up, her waist-beads slack, she always went to piss and he heard her. After that he liked to put his fingers deep in her wet bush and she crooned and grunted. He used to work for the Indians, moving boxes of stereo players from one shop to another, being told to step aside for Sanjay when he came in with his driver from his big house on the new estate. But they had sent him on weeks ago.

'My work is fine,' he said to her.

'And?'

'And what?'

'Your twins!'

'I don't know anything about these twins. How do I know they are mine?' he said sorely. His aunt had given him *pito* to drink last night.

'Don't be so foolish,' she said and cut the line.

He took some money from his aunt and walked through Rawlings Park. He set out to the *trotro* stop for Labadi Beach and soon enough pushed onto a revving bus. As the vehicle tore along Ring Road and some older ladies from Nungua began calling out to the driver to slow down, he knew inside of him that the twins were his own. Faustina said she had a tummy now, that you could see it was growing fast. She even felt them turning, squabbling, somersaulting like two small barracuda fish at sea. He jumped off at the beach and walked through the parking lot. He bought a beer at one of the bars, sitting down on a flaky white chair. He looked at his phone again. There were still no calls.

He watched the waves slapping on the sand, each one slightly different from the last. One fatter, one thin and dribbling at the top, then a rush of three at once. The water was grey like soup with no *wele* in it. He saw his twins' faces swimming inside of Faustina's fat stomach with its belly button thick and turned out. He would have to go back to the village and buy things for her. A bed for the little ones. Cloth for the naming ceremony. Minerals and money for the priest. But Sanjay had never given him his last pay. And now he was ashamed to go back to the Indians with their stereo sets in boxes, their fans with plastic bags tied over their tin basket heads. They had sent him on because there had never been any need for him in the first place, just to move aside when Sanjay came in with the driver, to check for thieves from the market, to move the boxes and fans from shop to shop or back inside at night.

An American girl came up to him and sat down. She was a dancer with the theatre, he knew her face. She bought him a beer and he rode back to town with her.

The French woman had told him many times over that her daughter Nathalie was a photographer in Paris. She had shown him black and white photos. They were of people staring back at her, people with long lives, old women in stuffed chairs, a man on a ladder. There was a woman in a park with a needle in her arm, her eyes black and lost and a dog waiting by her dirty feet. Her nipples pushed up through her T-shirt. A tree swept over her and a man glanced back but was already walking on to the apartment blocks after the fence. Mona was so proud of this shot. She said it had won a prize. But it left Montgomery in despair. *Why hadn't Nathalie called the hospital? Why was the woman outside in the cold with the waiting dog? Why was the man walking past to the buildings on the other side?* Mona had showed him other shots of men who were not men. His heart quickened when she showed him these. They were men with shaven heads and kohl around their eyes. Men in a bar grouped around a tiny Brazilian or half-blood man in a sparkling dress, who was hooting into the air. Afterwards they came into his head, these people. The drug addict and her dog, the Brazilian man in the dress, the old embattled white men with their makeup. They touched him and he wondered what Europe would be like: the wet parks with tall trees, the never-ending buildings and shops with their scrolls and windows, the faces cowering over him, giving him food and fucking him in the mouth, and he would look down and see he was wearing women's clothes.

He told Mona he wanted to marry her. Mona smiled at him, her long deep smile with the lip curving downward on one side into her furry *obroni* skin. He rubbed her nipple which grew taut like the woman in the photograph. He squeezed the small bud hard in his two fingers and watched her gasp.

I love you, Mona.

He walked back to Kojo's house. Kojo's brother was dying in hospital and there was no more hope to be had. The family wanted to take him back to the village to the fetish priests. Kojo sat on the steps and asked if the French woman would give him money. Montgomery shook his head.

'You go steal some?' Kojo suggested. 'You give her good *jiggy jiggy* and bitters and when she asleep then you go dollar dollar! I beg you man!'

But the idea returned to him later that evening when, after the *banku* and okra Kojo's aunt prepared for them, Mona called him on the telephone.

'*Allô* Montgomery. This is Mona. Can you hear me?'

Montgomery's stomach was so full he felt odd and light-headed. He couldn't talk.

'Montgomery? Is that you? Would you like me to call back another time?'

'Yes Madam,' he replied automatically while Kojo buried a laugh. 'I mean no, I am here. This is Montgomery here.'

'Are you okay?'

'Yes, yes Mona. I am fine.'

'Listen, this evening Miguel is sleeping over at his friend's house. Perhaps you can come over and we can talk of your twins. You know, if you want. I am here.'

He made a sign to Kojo to stop laughing but Kojo continued and Montgomery squashed his foot.

'Montgomery? Let me know, otherwise I'll go out. I don't feel like staying here alone tonight.'

'I am coming to you, Mona. You just wait I am coming.'

Kojo shook his head at him, his paw still in his soup, dribble on his chin.

Montgomery climbed the stairs. He was hard already in his jeans. His sweat prickled in his armpits and he thought he would shower first before they touched. The stairwell was always empty, with its smell of piss and Frytol, sweat and hair cream. There was no air except a violet flutter through the breeze-blocks at each landing, and this was corroded with shouting and fights. He wished he had shaved.

He pushed open the door and she was sitting at the computer wearing her reading glasses, dressed in a pair of shorts. He closed the door and walked inside, halting before he reached her, noting the cup of herbal tea with its ring of leaves and the steady European music. He felt disheartened, and stood still there. What would they speak about? He had told her about the twins, about how Faustina was his girlfriend at the village, and how she waited for him while he wanted to pull away.

'So Montgomery,' she said. 'You say you are becoming a father? What a surprise for you!'

'Yes.'

'Are we to celebrate?'

'Yes, of course.'

She went to the kitchen in her bare feet and brought forth two beers and the carved wooden coasters that he had given to her. She opened them and handed him one, bringing her bottle across to clink his on the neck. '*Félicitations!* So when are you going to your village?'

He did not answer her.

'You're not happy?'

'I want to stay with you.'

'But your children, Montgomery. Your bright new children. One moment, that's an email. It's Nathalie. She's coming out soon.'

Mona leant back over the computer, staring into the screen. He gulped down his drink and went to the kitchen for another. He opened the fridge, saw slabs of cheese and cartons of milk and sliced ham in a plastic packet, the beer and butter.

He went out onto the terrace. It was warm and windy in the night and immediately his thoughts grew darker. *If I threw myself down, she would suffer.* Then they would all know, even the son at school and the daughter in Paris. And they would send her away from the place where she worked.

He went back inside and she was fiddling with a camera, fitting in a reel of film and clasping the little door shut. She wound it on with a silver lever.

'Come, *mon amour*. I have an idea for you. Come into the bathroom.'

He let her lead him away. He thought of the people in her daughter's photographs as she removed his clothes. The haggard men dressed as women, the Brazilian man and the drug addict in the park. He sat on the cold floor cross-legged, balls and cock soft, head rolled backwards, nerves jostling. He heard the shutter as she began to snap. He closed his eyes. Then, slowly, ideas came to him and he began to move.

INNOCENT

By the time the vehicle reached the hilltop town of Sefwi Awiaso, Toby's lower back felt as though a small rock had somehow formed on the bone. The more she wriggled her bottom about the seat, the more the driver glanced at her from behind a pair of big, shoddy sun-glasses.

The road out of Sefwi Awiaso, down the other side of the hill where she was to work, had been built to resist three or four rainy seasons. Its destination was the recently completed cultural centre, an arched facility modelled on the Mediterranean style. Thereafter the road became stony and cantankerous, with deep gouges the forest pitted against. Girls wandering along with canisters on their heads had their intimacy stirred by the vehicle's passage.

The driver pulled into a hedged enclosure around a painted concrete block house. There was a short veranda, its floor lacquered in red oil paint and bearing two wicker chairs, with each window outlined in blue, all with newly repaired mosquito screens. The screens gave off a green glow in the falling light. A cat strode out, mewing for food.

The driver brought in her luggage. By this time Toby's back stung too much for her to pretend to assist. She was hungry although she wanted to suppress it. She unlocked the front door, praying the mirage would include a cold can of beer.

On the bench in the main room was an envelope with her full name written in heavy, loose letters. Toby had spoken at length with her predecessor, so these must have been the pointers dealing with the house and a quick run-down of the staff. While she read the page the driver settled himself at the screen door, hands crossed over his crotch like a mogul's bodyguard.

'What's your name?' Toby asked.

'Innocent, Madam.'

'You needn't call me Madam, Innocent. My name's Toby Vlaminck and you may call me Toby.'

'Yes, Madam Toby.'

She rolled her eyes. 'Have it your way then.'

He was too tall for the shirt someone had given him. His trousers were rather more hopeful of reaching his ankles. In his battered sandals were bluey black feet etched in chalk, then delicate, shell-tinged nails. He jangled the keys, not liking her perusal.

'Are you married, Innocent? Do you have a family?'

'No, Madam Toby. I have a girl and she be waiting for a baby. We marry after.'

'That's good for you, Innocent. Make sure you marry her.'

When he left Toby ran a cold can of beer along her back. There was no hot water. The muscles had locked together and if she turned in a certain way a terrible pronging went forth through her bottom and thigh and tugged the entire network of her back.

She slept remembering the crummy film she saw on the plane out.

The driver, Innocent, was often superfluous. He reported for work each morning at seven-thirty. Toby heard him call through the back window to the cook, before he walked the ten or so paces to the red painted veranda and stepped inside to salute her solemnly. He then went out and sat in the car, his large head slumping backwards as he dozed. According to her predecessor's sketch, Innocent was *a born-again kleptomaniac who hopped in and out of the sack*. For complete loyalty, it was recommended to *buy him the hugest showiest pair of Peter Fonda sun-glasses you can get your hands on, at least once a year.*

Each month it was necessary to see how the various micro-projects in the surrounding villages were faring. These included a primary school, a toilet block, a market place and a furnace for making roof tiles. The projects were all at the stage where they were run solely by locals. Toby was the only white in the area and felt the ripple her visits made in the villages.

On one of these occasions Innocent returned to the car and asked Toby if they could bring a woman back to town with them. The woman he indicated was standing at his side, short and ill-looking. She wore a headscarf that made her ears protrude unnaturally, that made one want to fix it for her. Innocent explained that she was his wife.

'You mean the woman who will become your wife?'

He lowered his eyes and said that she was losing his baby.

The trip back to Sefwi Awiaso passed through a rich virgin forest the government had harnessed from timber cutters. Isolated trees rose from the noisy undergrowth to astonishing heights. Calls shot the humid silence. A trembling black mamba slithered across the road.

Although Innocent had said the girl could speak no English Toby turned around repeatedly, especially once when she was sure she heard a cry of pain. Against the upholstery, the girl had begun to look much younger than she had seemed at her lover's side, surrounded by a mesh of women with babies and small children cradled in their laps.

'How old is your girlfriend?'

'She be sixteen.'

'Are you sure? Does her family know what has happened?'

'No – if her father know he be very angry. He kill me.'

'How many months is she?'

'She tell me three months, maybe four. She take a drink they give to young girls.'

'You mean she wanted to abort?'

'She be young, Madam Toby. Unless she take it her father kill me.'

Toby's head went blank with anger. She whipped around, jerking her back, thus sending a spurt of heated fuzziness up and down her flank.

The girl had fainted.

Three or four days later Innocent came and told her that the girl had gone home and that in order to make peace with the family he would have to finance a wedding as soon as possible. He asked Toby for a large advance on his pay, quite eloquently. Toby gave him the money and a heavy talking down, during which tears appeared below his Peter Fonda sun-glasses. Innocent disappeared for two weeks when she presumed the wedding took place and came back looking uncomfortably refreshed.

AT THE MALGA

At dawn Marco left. She heard the crampons clinking in his knapsack and the slide of buckle straps pulled tight. The empty sock of his helmet against a thigh. To her each movement sounded groggy but she knew Marco was thinking with absolute clarity. There was a fringe of light around the window, she was stiff. Marco opened the door and the curtain banked inward, expiring. He would have done one more round of the room, he was gone.

It was cold. She heard other hikers trooping down the stairs, their equipment clanking and swishing, as noisy as they were voiceless. Though she wished she could go back to sleep she saw them with puffy eyes and unruly hair downing coffee at the restaurant, in a group at a single table where the Romanian girl had lain out a fresh cloth. The Italians would have been the loudest. Not Marco though, in the mornings he was morose. He would have singled out a stern-looking local, a man he could look up to, follow perhaps, to see this thing through. They would wordlessly set out from the lodge, trudging in time along the first paths. It was important to establish a rhythm, a code for the ascension. Others would film the peak's chilly heights but their heads would be bent down as though transfixed.

Veronique pulled across the cover from Marco's bunk. It was an old frayed goose down quilt that smelt of being stowed away. She heard two more stragglers shunting down the stairs, whose boots sounded lighter on the wood. They must have been the two Spanish women they had spoken to last night, Marco so reluctant to become their beacon for the trek. Well, he had escaped them. She waited for the light to unfurl on their belongings and saw the last of the dried fruit in a sachet, the wrapper of an energy bar he must have consumed in the dark. She reached up to draw the curtain behind her and the room buzzed with unfiltered, bursting light. She turned on her belly and saw the opposite peak looming. The light brought it closer, so that the dimensions gave way to its sharp, agitated pixels.

Yesterday's trek had been hard for her. Initially, she took the ski-lift from the car park while Marco set out at a half-jog to the top of the first ridge. She recognised the bearded mountain boy tending the lift from last winter. She felt a flutter. But the young man had no memory of her. It felt so silly without skis, without the slippery ice. Without hearing the beep of her ski pass as she neared the turnstile. She handed over her money and tip-toed through the mud. She walked up to the shabby conveyor belt. Behind her, each pair of seats swung around the pylon at the bottom of the course and set off against the texture of the mountain. Next to her, the boy jerked up the metal footrest so that it hit the pole dangling from the cable. He slowed the moving seat an instant while she lowered her buttocks.

She eased onto the scarred plastic and the lift trundled away on its lonely climb. She saw Marco from above. He was weaving through the summer grass, he had found a dry path away from the swamp at the bottom of the valley. The cable thrummed through the cogs at the top of the first pylon and her seat jolted. Marco didn't see her. She checked her rucksack for her sun-glasses and put them on. Below, the water was stagnant and brown where last winter there had been a blue-white mantle, hardly touched by the sun. But now the earth was rank and sunken, it seemed the water never receded, and the cut swathe of the ski slope was pitted with ruts and grassy clumps. Over to the right, where the valley rose, there were cow pats and a false smoother greenness, a slotted wooden fence along the road to the pass.

The cable pulled upward at the next pylon and Veronique looked at the twisted steel wire in motion, travelling against the still sky. Ahead of her, the empty seats ascended. She could see a pair of youngsters close to the top, their boots kicking and an occasional laugh dropping into the air and falling towards her. She knew the climb would take twenty minutes, though it would seem a good deal longer, such was the contrast with the spare alpine world at the top. Now her feet seemed to skim the tips of pine trees where their vigour was apparent, also the trickiness of the terrain. Oblong-shaped rocks slid where they wished, along with severed trunks matted with moss. She saw a lean creature turn towards her through the trees, looking into her eyes before it disappeared. In a broad rubbishy trail she saw the winter's litter – ski gloves, ski poles, beanies, cigarette packets and chewing gum wrappers. The detritus of a huge beast that had lumbered off, beeped the car alarm of its Cayenne and torn the landscape with a roil of diesel fumes.

She had lost sight of Marco. Once she thought she heard his rhythmic *pad-pad-pad* as he jogged, but she wasn't certain. There were so few sounds now that the wind had picked up, harsh and cool on her cheeks and blowing her hair over her face. She was high enough now to see the surrounding peaks. Denuded, rent by shadow, when in winter they were masses of snowy light. She knew why those who had the gumption and resources hired helicopters to deposit them up there, to ski down in powerful ruddered curves, minutiae on the mountain folds. It brought the soul to the surface, into the crackling air. When she was a young woman she had tried it once and it had scared the shit out of her.

She washed her face, dressed and went down for a coffee. Seeing the debut elements of Marco's trek made her restless. Her knee warmed and loosened by degrees, though the hike after yesterday's lift ride had inflamed the tendons again, and she hadn't rested well. She sat on the wooden deck of the lodge with a second coffee, peering over the town squeezed at the base of the peaks. She could have stayed down there, bedded at a friend's, gone mushroom-hunting in the woods. She could have gone for an aperitif at the *enoteca* with a crowd she knew, and watched the change of tide at the summer's end as the last tourists closed their shutters and filled their cars with suitcases and children. She watched the Romanian woman gather up beer glasses and cigarette butts left outside last night. Seeing the younger woman made her think of Marco in a crude way, atop her. She let the image roll, feeling an unkind voyeurism.

A grey-haired man came outside and greeted the foreign woman. He too carried a coffee to the bench and succumbed to the colossal views. It truly was a panoramic day, pencilled out by the gods. He came and sat by Veronique.

'Not up for the big hike?' he said. 'If I'm not mistaken I heard you speaking English last night.'

'Yes, that's right. It's a long-standing stalemate situation. We were both students in England. Neither of us willing to perfect the other's language.'

'And you are?'

'Veronique.' They shook hands. 'A recycled academic wriggling through the Italian system. Yourself?'

He laughed. 'Heinrik. Pleasure. A lowly accountant visiting a sister marooned in the valley here. I come from just outside Nuremburg.'

'And your excuse for not joining the excursion?'

'Pure laziness, I'll confess. I'm here with my brother-in-law and drank rather a lot last night. When the alarm went off this morning I just turned over and refused to move. Alfredo was furious with me. I'm not sure how I'll redeem myself.'

He finished off his coffee and placed the cup on the saucer, rolling up the empty sugar sachet into a ball.

'Not that I mind the idea of doing nothing for a day. The drive down here was hell. I've had car problems you wouldn't dream of. So why no walk for you, Veronique?'

She threw back the rest of the coffee, wishing she had accepted a nip of grappa at the bar. 'I had a rather stupid skiing accident this winter. A beginner put her ski under mine and sent me over as we got off the lift. I tore tendons and spent the season on crutches. I'm not sure hiking up here yesterday was such a good idea. We do this peak every year at this time before the great wade back to work.'

'Your husband's gone up?'

'He's a keen climber.'

There was a silence which Veronique assumed indicated the absence of a wife or partner.

'Would you mind if I ordered another coffee? I have quite a banging head.'

'No problem.'

He walked back inside and she wondered how the day might unfold. She had no wish to hike by herself. Her knee was too tender and at most she could make it to the lake just beyond the lodge. Anything else would not only be foolish, it might compromise her return to the car tomorrow morning. Marco had an appointment the next day with a doctorate student who had bottomed out. He had needed this break after a complex year of caring for an ill mother and her own useless months on crutches.

Heinrik came out with a steaming cup of coffee and sat down. It was then that she saw the right side of his face had a burns scar that reached his ear. It was an old wound that the skin had tried to hem in, but the tissue remained thick and twisted.

'I don't expect they'll be in until around four or five,' Heinrik said.

'Yes.'

A mother led her children out onto the deck, two eight or nine-year-old twins and a young teenager. The kids began to banter, while the older child hunched down with an iPod, her eyes heavily outlined. In their wake a tanned handsome father sauntered down the stairs dressed in hiking gear. Veronique turned away from the group back to the spinning views, sensing Heinrik's eyes upon her.

141

'So how is the injured knee bearing up this morning?'

'It's stiffer than I'd like. Yesterday's walk was quite punishing.'

Throughout these slow months of recovery many doubts had visited her. There were days when she hadn't gone to work but had stayed in the apartment, immobile, tasting pain and decline. There were times when Marco had rejected her. When her helplessness caused him aggravation, which hadn't softened. That was why she had tried so hard on the last part of the walk yesterday. Reaching the lodge had been momentous.

But today her knee hurt. 'I think I would love a tiny shot of grappa, if you don't mind.'

Heinrik came out with two glasses as the family trailed off behind the building, up the path towards the lake. Many groups never made it past this location where there were stretches of soft grass and overturned rocks providing shade. There were *stelle alpine* in crannies and the lake's clear water shirred under gusts of cool wind. Picnic rugs were spread out, couples snogged and children went exploring. Other paths continued around the north face, but these were scored in the frozen rockslide beneath the peak. Edgy and wind-whipped, these were rigorous walks.

'Thank you, that was lovely.' She twisted around to the summit that Marco and the group of hikers were attempting today. By now they would be ascending shallow rock trails etched into the high ridges, careful not to dislodge stones that would hurtle onto those below, rarely looking upward into the stringent air. She wished she were with him. How easy it was to imagine her sturdy footfalls and the occasional drift of her husband's scent! That she was here and not there seemed part of a mesh of untrue realities. She had never been disabled before, nor seen such vexation in Marco's eyes. Why had she toppled over when that idiotic English student had jammed a ski beneath hers? Why hadn't she righted herself, or pulled away sooner, before hitting the ice as a hot spasm sliced through her knee?

'Are you planning on going for a walk?' she asked Heinrik.

'I'm in no rush to do anything, quite truthfully.' He made a strange, distasteful expression with his face. 'Given the effort it took to get up here – we arrived extremely late to find the kitchen doors barred – I'm not sure I could attempt more than a non-athletic wander.'

'I'm not sure I'm even up for that.'

The black-eyed teenager came stomping back onto the wooden deck and stood fuming over the precipice. Her father followed, braking slightly when he took in Heinrik and Veronique. As they began to argue in Italian, Heinrik spoke to her. 'Do you have some sort of anti-inflammatory drugs or cream? Perhaps we could attempt a slow walk. There is a *malga* beyond the lake and I'd like to buy some cheese to take home. It is not so far. And surely it is best to avoid this,' he said, indicating the quarrelling pair.

Veronique had seen the *malga* on a velvet green hollow strewn with rocks from the great mountain. Marco had never wanted to go there and it had not occurred to her. 'Of course, yes. We could do that. Shall we leave now?'

She limped up to her room and gathered her jacket and walking stocks, throwing down two painkillers with a tetrapack of mango juice. When she returned to the deck the young girl sat sullen on a bench in the shadow, her father staring at his boots. Heinrik stood there eating a roll, and watched her approach more expectantly than she might have wished. His trunk was long and his stocky legs were quite short; she had noticed a plump backside. The thatch of fused skin twitched in the light.

'Are we ready then?' He looked at her sternly. 'I hope I'm not pushing you too hard.'

'Not at all,' she replied. 'I wouldn't have known what to do with myself.'

As they walked they did not speak. She lagged behind on the first climb towards the trail around the lake. He waited at the top, peering over the other side, without watching her progress. She was glad to be moving. Some sort of internal sap greased her knee and it seemed alive again, either the grappa or the pills. She felt forgiven for the exasperating effort yesterday. This would be an easier walk, without Marco setting the pace. By the time she reached the crest her body had warmed through and the ragged air wove into her lungs. She felt vital, her body quavered.

The lake lay below them cupped in a shoulder of the ridge. Icy blue, riffed by wind, the path around it was already dotted with morning walkers commencing the trail to the north. Some of them stood bedazzled by the sunlight, amassed in a crucible before the shadows of the cold wall. Veronique felt the friction of light over her skin, or was it the wind outlining her? At such a slow walking pace the mountain had already assumed a different geometry, less straining and more rotund, its concaves absorbent.

'You're rather a strong walker,' Heinrik observed.

'Yes.'

Veronique had never paused here this long, except to loosen her neck scarf or apply sunblock. But now she felt an urge to wade into the rippled surface, feeling her bare feet fitting over the round stones and the chill delineation rising along her thighs. She wondered what would happen if she were to shed her clothes before poor Heinrik here, and proceed into the water.

'Are you having mad thoughts?' he detected.

'Quite,' she said.

He moved on and she followed him towards a path that disregarded the lake and set out to the west. After the first twists and rocky steps it ascended steeply. She expanded her intake of breath and heard Heinrik's level gasps. The knee that had soured her last few months now felt feisty and repaired. She kept pace with the German and was not far behind him when they reached the cusp which marked a passage into the next slim valley. They both throbbed at the top. Nestled in the green was a stone hamlet surrounded by a group of cows.

'You say you've never been here?'

Veronique shook her head.

'Here, why don't you take this?' He handed her a knotted stick that another walker had placed in a cleft in the rocks. It was the right height for her.

They began to stagger downward. Every few steps she was aware of the pulleys behind her kneecap, stretching and subsiding, but she braced her leg muscles, trying to calibrate the discomfort before it became an insoluble pain. She wondered if the drugs had already worn off and felt for the blister pack of pills in her pocket. Perhaps the people at the *malga* would provide them with a jug of wine. She watched Heinrik's uneven movements for a few seconds and realised she would portray him to her husband as a marred, colourless man. She pushed on, feeling guilty. It was an unexpected, regretful thought.

'Shall we rest a little? There's no reason to rush,' Heinrik said, turning up towards her. Behind him, the small building sat like a child's sketch on the rich, saturated landscape. She smelt a whiff of dung, and then the creamy stink of cheese.

Soon enough Heinrik stood beneath the stone door lintel, waiting for her last steps along the broadened trail. Cows looked over her in mild surprise, with their geography of bounty and production. A carved wooden bench sat against the wall in the sun.

Heinrik beckoned her into the darkness of the hut where her eyes fumbled to retrieve vision. She smelt embers burning. She stepped onto a stone floor. She made out two rooms, one with a large central fireplace beneath a funnel dropped from the ceiling. Two long branches were interlocked at one point where a burning scission occurred, heating the space in a way that seemed selfless.

In the second room tablets of glowing yellow cheese lay on wooden shelves. There were four rows of these emerging into the sombre light. Later, the woman would place one in her hands, like the nourishment from a stark tabernacle.

Heinrik guided her to the woman sitting in the window bay. She may have been Veronique's age, her hair was wiry and her face split with lines. At first Veronique shuddered. The woman seemed an ignorant cave dweller, pensive at the window, guarding her crop. Her eyes fell upon them abrasively.

Heinrik stepped forward. Veronique watched the light from the fireplace travel over his back and the jarring this produced in his shoulders as the warmth took hold. He glanced behind at the blue flickers. The scar tissue on the side of his face now appeared in relief, its vicious origin no longer falsified by healing. Veronique came closer, touched his spine, placed herself between the man's body and the flames.

JANET AND THE ANGRY TREES

As far as I am aware, the first-born son is a source of jubilation in every culture. When Luca brings me to his parents' house I expect this to be so, but it is not the case.

Luca drives up to an old farmhouse next to a ditch running along the roadside, with a crooked iron gate clinging to its post. Four tall old trees are pressed to the house. They are a strange tree I have never seen before. The branches twist out with spiny blue growth that is not leaves at all, just angry digits.

The front door is open.

Luca swears and leaves the car revving when he lifts out. *'Non ci credo, non ci credo,'* he says. We are here because he wants to offer me employment. I told him I know old people, my grandmother was old and we looked after her.

Luca trudges off and I look over the vegetable garden. Straining towards the sun is the streaky white-boned spinach they have here, and tossed purple cabbage heads trapped in the dirt. I am not disappointed. We have all left behind our pasts.

Luca comes back out and turns off the car. He lunges across and kisses me, but there is acid in his mouth, he is tense.

'Okay, let's go.'

I set down my heels in the gravel and smooth my hair, testing my smile in the air. Every shaky step I take after him is a step towards a new life, and my new lives have been numerous now. I walk into the darkened hallway and follow him to the rear of the house. In a cramped putrid kitchen two battered old white people are sitting at a table. The woman wears kooky glasses on her nose. The tall prickly-skinned man breathes noisily through his throat.

'Janet dear, meet my parents, Pietro and Valentina. They are very pleased to meet you.'

I put out my hand which the woman takes greedily, her

lilac fingers closing like chicken wings. The old man grabs my hand and puts his other palm somewhere south of my belt, squeezing fruit. I see my lover's face lodged within his, the way that when two dogs mate you see snatches of the parent.

Luca is at the empty kitchen counter opening a bottle, putting down four glasses, filling them with blood-red wine. I do not drink except on occasion, but Luca puts a glass into my hand and gulps down himself. The two old people look at their glasses oddly, then the old man slurps his wine back.

I see Luca is embarrassed but in my village it is the same. The old people snort and fart and cackle like the babies we pin to our backs. The old men watch young girls parading to the well. The breasts of the old women are empty skins on their bellies with swinging knots.

Luca turns on the television set. 'Everything works here. It's simple, but everything works. The washing machine is in the next room, though you won't need to iron. My father is in the garden or the work shed all day. My mother, well, she can't see to clean anymore and she wanders off. I've told you about that. Come upstairs and I'll show you your room.'

He carries my suitcase up the stone stairs.

'Here, it's my old room. I grew up here,' he says, shaking his head.

I press myself to his front but his embrace is rapid and thin.

'No Janet, not here. I couldn't possibly.'

He looks at me with a paltry, stirred face. It is his going-home face, when I know that he has already left me.

'I'll be out before the weekend with some shopping. Now let me head off.'

I hear the front door close and the revving of his car outside. He backs into the lane and drives away, banishing us all from his head. I have passed his home in the new housing estate, far from the city ring road where he picks me up. I am happy to know he has a good wife and a handsome young son.

As I unpack my things I hear Luca's father breathing hoarsely at my bedroom door. That I do not understand his language so well does not bother me. He is an old man. An old man deserves comfort after the trials of life. He speaks to me in a ravaged voice as I push Luca's coats to one side and hang up my leather jacket, the one his son gave to me.

'I don't understand you, Grandfather. In a minute I'll be downstairs to prepare some soup.'

He stands there watching me as I try to decipher one of Luca's framed certificates on the wall.

'Off you go then, let me put on some other clothes.'

But he won't budge when I push the door and stays staring. I strip down, ease out of my heels, pull on slacks and a Chinese top, put on some jute slippers.

'Was that fun, Grandfather? Now let us get some dinner.'

I move past him in the doorway and take his hand to lead him down the stairs. His hand is wrapped in heavy veins and the skin is rough. He jerks it away and holds it to his chest. I leave him and make my way to the kitchen.

Over the empty stone sink there are patterned brown tiles and a row of cupboards. Luca's mother is still sitting at the table, her hand reaching out but just shy of the wineglass. I go over and hold it to her mouth. She smiles at me. Her eyes are the most beautiful blue-grey, it is the same blue-grey as the angry trees. I tip some wine into her mouth and let her savour and swallow. Through the window I see a tilled field with a small tractor parked halfway down in the mud. The shiny steel tooth of the plough rests inside the earth. Luca's father reaches the kitchen door and snarls across the room unkindly. I put down the glass. His tiny wife has a dribble on her chin.

He moves over and turns up the television even louder. There are dancing girls on the screen. Lovely, pretty women with full bottoms and high breasts like teenage girls. They dance with each other, the audience claps hard. There are two normal people sitting in the middle whose faces are nervous. It makes me happy, it seems like a type of ceremony.

I lie down in Luca's bed and turn over and over. His parents lie asleep across the hallway like two children who have played all afternoon, their covers clutched as they whisper and snuffle. The man's long feet reach out for those of the tiny woman and they interlock. But their faces are turned away to each side of the night. Through the small windows moonlight sifts inside. I have left my window open so I can smell the land and the trees. It is a warm, wet smell that is alive. A car races past, whipping along, music caught inside. I know it is a man driving from the way he has no care for anyone but himself. I think of showing my thatch on the side of the road, the cash afterwards, walking home with my back aching.

Luca told me his wife's name is Barbara. She is Scottish and her pregnancy was difficult. First the tests he told me about briefly, then months of bed rest. I used to think of the vigilant wife with her loins clamped shut, the infant like a small device lolling in her violet waters. After the birth there had been trouble, haemorrhage, the misfortune of her dry breasts. Luca had been so vexed. Barbara, by contrast, seemed like a friend to me. She seemed worthy.

I think of my sister Faustina whose twins died inside of her. How the blackness came about and the smell of rot that came from her mouth. How small and clean her body became in the morgue before we buried her. And the babies' faces clean as fists in the casket.

The night is stretching out and I can hear the old people tossing in their sleep. I think of Luca embracing the Scottish woman's white back, kissing the lovely pearls of her vertebrae. I feel Faustina's arms clutching me, pulling me back. *Don't let me die, Janet. Don't let me die!* I hear the old man go to piss and then come fumbling with my door handle. His memory is sharp, he won't pass peacefully.

It is a beautiful morning. Near the river, the mist used to gather like this in my own village. Across the fields there is a mountain cut at the base by a thick white line. In a way, I don't want it to leave us. For the day to become bright and distinct. Downstairs Luca's mother is in the kitchen making coffee. Beneath the old colonnade attached to the house I hear her husband hitting metal against metal. I try speaking to Luca's mother, finding a way into the jumble of her mind. She turns to me as though we have been sisters forever, as though she knows Faustina's agony and the bliss seeped into the dead twins' faces.

There is nothing of Luca in her.

We sit at the table to drink our coffee together. On the cool marble there is a bowl of beans to be shelled. They are the fat pink beans they grow here. She takes up a long pod and runs her finger down the seam, spilling the fruit into a second empty bowl. I do the same. We continue to do this until the first bowl is full of skins and the next full of bright, expectant beans.

Later, I shower quickly in the bathroom downstairs. The water is cool, the shower recess hosts ridges of mould and grime. It has the smell of something buried. I doubt the Scottish woman has ever been here. I scrub my skin hard with the brush my mother sends to me. My skin burns and shines afterwards. Women from our place have hard, plump skin.

Out in the kitchen I smell gas. The woman has put the beans in a pot of water without lighting the flame. I open the windows and back door and shoo away the odour, my hair dripping and my towel flapping. Luca's mother trots up to the doorway. She looks interested and pleased.

'Grandma, watch out! Your son will beat me if you should burn the house down!'

I light the flame under the pot and she appears to have

151

moved onto another thought.

When I am dressed we sit together in front of the house in the spaces between the angry blue trees. She suns herself, her legs falling apart. I see she is wearing an itchy sweater which she tugs at her neck. She removes this and sits happily in the sun in an old brassière, her breasts falling either side of her ribs. She points to my silver sun-glasses I stole from a man's car and I hand these over.

In a while she is dozing and I wander back through the house. The front rooms catch the light but they are disused. In one room there is an exercise machine and a bookshelf with a set of encyclopedias. The second has a dining table that has been waxed. It is obvious that Luca's parents prefer the kitchen at the back with the new television and the furniture huddled close. It is right that they have their broken armchairs and radio sets. I notice there are no framed photographs anywhere. No brides in the church garden, no babies in shawls. My first European – this was in Germany – he used to bring me to his home where there were many photographs. His wife looked very stern, as though she made sure all things were perfect.

Just before noon I hear Luca's special call on the mobile phone in my jeans' pocket. I rush outside into the sunlight. My heart levers in my chest and my stomach feels vacant.

'My darling!' I say to him.

'How are they? Are they behaving? Don't let my father put on the heating. There's absolutely no need for it. I hope you haven't been, er, shocked.'

'When are you coming to see me?'

'That'll be soon. Don't let my mother go wandering off to the village. Or start trying to flag down cars.'

'You know you have no worries with me, my honey.'

'I know that, Janet.'

'Won't you say something sweet to me?'

'Janet, there'll be time for that. I'm picking up Barbara

now from work. On Saturday she needs to photograph the house. You'll have to go somewhere. I'll drop you at the station. We've got to get the plans through for when they're gone. Oh dammit –'

'Luca?'

'That was the police. Look, I'd better get off this thing. Thursday afternoon is good for me. I might take you to the hills.'

'Luca, I want to suck your cock.'

'Don't talk like that, Janet. You know you don't have to talk like that.'

'I know you are hard in your pants. I know you are.'

'Fuck it Janet, *will you stop this.*'

The old man is standing behind me in the shadow of one of the trees. I remove the silver sun-glasses and urge Luca's mother to get dressed.

Luca's mother is a sound and able cook. Her giddiness dispels and the food she produces is accomplished, leaving one longing for just a mouthful more. Her husband eats like a man who hasn't eaten in months. I finish my plate and the taste makes a lather all the way to my gut. I lick my lips and drink a half-glass of wine. The old man turns on the television and the dancing girls appear, shaking and trembling across the screen. Luca's mother, she looks lost, as though she has just walked in and we are new to her. I stand up and put the dishes in the sink. She grasps my waist and hugs me like a contented girl.

Upstairs the cupboards are full of musty shirts and trousers, piles of creased leather shoes. I drag the mats downstairs and throw them over the fence, hitting them with a broom. In the laundry I find a vacuum cleaner which I use in the rooms upstairs. I spray the windows, wiping them down with spit and the pages of an old sports newspaper. For a while Luca's mother follows me, then I see her nestled on the bed, shoes on and mouth open, a fly circling her head. I put down my rag and spray and walk into her room. I sit down. I lie out next to her and listen to her breathing. Everything about her is thinned away and filled with lightness. If she becomes any smaller she will be able to turn around and begin her life again.

When I have finished the upstairs rooms I go into the kitchen and make myself a cup of Liptons. I think of Luca as a child here, asking for milk or playing with the new fresh beans. Or whimpering under the table after lashings with the father's belt. He is right to ensure that his handsome son will not have the same impoverished life. He is right to have moved on, to have married the Scottish wife and bought the neat house on the estate. He is right - these people will die off and then they can cut down the trees and fix the gate. This can be a lovely farmhouse, sold for good money like the ones up the road, with perhaps a restaurant under the colonnade at the side. I think of Luca driving towards me on the ring road, quickly pulling the car away in the dark, the other girls strutting and cooing. How proud he is with his dashboard full of lights, how he likes to be rough in the trees, how he wipes his face and checks his phone with grief afterwards. My mother used to say it was better that it was Faustina who went. Faustina was lazy and had gotten with child fast. In the end, even Fausty knew. It is true my mother groomed me for a life of diligence.

I hear a rumbling at the crooked gate. It is not Luca's big car. It is another small tractor like the one out the back stuck in the field. I stand at the doorway squinting in the sun. This stone house is so cold within.

It is another old farmer with a hat and a set of braces pulled over his shrunken shoulders and round belly. Luca's father has ambled over to the gate carrying a stick. He waves it in the air as he talks over the engine. He points to me in the doorway and the driver tilts his hat back to peer, lifting his chin and stretching his pale neck. I wave to them. They continue to stare my way. I know that old people can be kindly, but often they look at us as though we have stolen from their homes and their lives.

154

But it is not their fault. They know they piss like babies and the time has come for them to leave.

Midway through the afternoon the clanging sound recommences from beneath the colonnade. I know that Luca's mother still sleeps upstairs. Outside, the old man doesn't see me watching from behind a plant with washed dark green leaves. He is hitting a tool on the long workbench and there are sparks. His frailty has dispersed and the muscles under his shirt look nourished and young. His lips are peeled open showing his aligned false teeth.

When I go back inside Luca's mother is gone. I pull out my telephone ready to call the son, but back off. Barbara. *I'm picking up Barbara now from work.* A tender afternoon with some seductive sex. He told me that's what they do together. *My wife is a seductive woman.* I charge out onto the road, not yet calling the mother's name. I spin around. The road is empty. I can't lose my chance to please him.

I stumble around the back of the house to the muddy field cast in northern shadow. The air is damp, somehow a cold wind collects here. I run the length of the colonnade and back, then bolt across to the front of the farmhouse again, where shadows from the angry trees extend in tilted strips. On the other side of the house there is only the ragged vegetable patch.

I jog past the blue-grey trees as the clanging begins to hurt my chest. I have lost her. I can't go on. Luca will kill me. A gluey smell comes from the trees as they run their lace over my cheeks. At the base of the furthest tree I see her crouched in the soil, a naked woman like a bundle of sticks.

It is Luca's own mother squatting like a child, her broad feet half-buried and her woman's parts plunged into the fresh dirt. She has rubbed clots into her hair so that it is dark and thick as my own. On her body, her fingers have drawn wet brown welts across her trunk and over her slack bosoms. Her brown face smiles under the blue drift of the tree.

I bend to her, take her hand.
I clasp the woman tighter, and tighter.

WHERE THE WOUNDED GO

He remembered the bite. It must have been an insect in the kitchen. Or on the porch with its wall of hairy leaves. It happened the week Henry was away – something about timber – and he knew a part of his mother was already in pain, had known that it would come for her. The day after it was pink; three days later there was a strip of red heat between the knuckles on her empty ring finger and the wound puckered open with green lips.

He watched her in the bathroom, dabbing it with alcohol, the dirty strip of gauze on the floor. It was her face that he watched.

'Blimey,' his mother said. 'I didn't think a finger could hurt as much.'

She was naked, they were always naked in that house, even Henry with his thingy and high bottom where you could see the muscles shift. It was him who pushed the old walking stick against the bedroom door to keep them out.

She pulled over her cloth and bunched it under her arm.

'Why you looking at me like that, hon? Where's Kwesi? Go and see what Kwesi's doing out the back.'

He could smell the dry alcohol, it was like the strong flowers on the fence. One afternoon when his mother and Henry weren't home he had opened the bottle and breathed in hard. Now she yelped a little, her hand squeezing tight around the finger wrapped in white cotton wool, the alcohol dripping on her thighs and running onto the floor as she braced. When he was small he had fallen from a wooden castle in a park back at home. He had fallen sideways, landed on his ribs, gotten winded. As he dropped he saw her beginning to sprint, her face stretched out in a horrible shape. He had thought that he would always feel her in his tissue.

'For God's sake, Blake! Can't you hear your brother

screaming? Get out of here and do something!'

He hoped that Henry never came back.

It was true that Kwesi was screaming. But it was his 'afraid' cry, he hadn't hurt himself. Probably threw a piece of glass at the dogs when they wrinkled their lips at him. They never did that with Blake. Blake hit the screen door leading outside, walked down the painted red steps and dipped his shoulder just in time before the door thwacked against the house. Kwesi's body was thrown back on the dirt between the plantains and he was howling. The dogs looked at Blake from the doorless, roofless shed pushed against the fence, their tails thumped on the hot concrete.

'Kwesi, shut up. Stop crying,' Blake said. 'Where's Agnes?'

Agnes was always in the driver Ibrahim's room in the boys' quarters, cooing and curling herself on his bed. She never looked after them. Blake walked over and stood above Kwesi. For a moment his baby brother stopped crying, enough time to see who it was standing over him. Then he started again, his bubbly brown eyes squeezing shut and producing tears.

'Can't you bloody well pick him up?'

It was his mother shouting from the back door, which she shoved open, running down as the door slapped, the poisoned finger stuck out in front as she rushed over with bare, blue-nailed feet. Her other arm swept under Kwesi's back and scooped him up. It was true there was a piece of broken glass clutched in his hand. She put him on her hip and went back inside scolding, throwing down the glass. The dogs watched, looking happier with the quiet.

Blake looked up at the plantain trees, how they seemed like men in yellow and green jackets. There was no fruit. The landlord came and took it first, the big green chandeliers. He and Henry had had a loud fight over that. Henry had come crashing back into the house, knocking things, feeling big. His mother grew angry too, it was a new turbulent kind of anger that made her body heave and her eyes grow into slits as she followed him about the house and they drank beers together sitting on the back steps, telling Blake and the other kids to go back inside. The building next door was empty. It was big with many storeys and broken windows although in some you could see people and smell fish frying at night. The gate onto the street was always locked. Henry said he would take Blake to the top which was flat and from there you could see the whole city, to the sea and the hills and back. Though it made his mother smile and trace her finger along Henry's neck, Blake and Henry looked at each other and they both knew he never would.

His mother was feeding Kwesi on the couch. Kwesi's body was sucked into hers, his foot kicking and one hand searching for her other brown nipple, tugging it, which she didn't even notice. She closed her eyes. Her wet sandy hair stuck to her forehead and the lines there twitched. The bandaged finger was thrown away from her, the hand lay half-clasped on its back.

'Blake, get me some water, will you please? I think this thing has given me fever.'

'Why don't you go to the doctor?'

'I think I'll have to. Henry's sister works at the clinic. Maybe you could get me something at the chemist. God knows where Agnes has gotten to.' She groaned. 'I don't understand. It's really throbbing now, it was just a scratch.'

'Why don't you call Henry?' Blake said. For that was what his mother wanted to hear, Henry's name in his mouth.

'Henry's fucking phone is off. I can't handle this any longer.'

She began to sob. Kwesi detached to look at the awful, ragged crying coming from her, then grabbed her teat again, easing its long flesh into his mouth. Blake had stopped thinking that she might ever abandon the pair of them – Kwesi and Henry – who she had brought to the centre of their lives. He and his brother and sister were part of a contagion that always dragged behind her.

He brought her water. He picked up Kwesi and burped him on his back, leaving her alone. He and Kwesi ate a banana on the steps.

She moved away from Henry's body, unstuck her skin, as if there were a true adhesion. She ran her fingers over his rump, into the lovely crevice that was hers for keeps. It was never enough. The gulping, the way he sired her, it had never been done, she was almost sure of it. Henry murmured and she clung to him. If she thought of him with another woman she could sense a scalding ghastliness. With Dean she had known that there was a pulsing part of her that he had never even touched or triggered in the dark.

Kissing Henry Osei that night in the dirty Havana Bar, it had been a revelation. That man and woman could exchange such compassion, leading to such bottomless depths. But the gluey genitals, swollen and fused, that was not what it was about. She'd tried to tell Dean it wasn't an affair, it was *a communion*. In the early days, stuffed with guilt, she had even tried the sex on Dean, to see if it might transfer. But Dean had loved it for all the wrong reasons. *I love fucking you like this, this is so fucking erotic. Oh baby I love the way you –*

Oh God! Where Henry had positioned her to be saved. He had never, ever insisted. He said, *If you want to be with me, I will give you the world, a new world, all of you. That means your kids.*

Her pregnancy had been almost immediate and Kwesi's birth had been nothing less than spiritual. She still replayed it in her mind, told it to other open-mouthed women. The baby sliding into her hands, chalky and velvet, her natural kneeling position, the massive orgasm of expulsion. Then the other children piled around her in the clinic room. It had been her greatest achievement, and Henry so proud.

I've earned this. I love you. I love what you have given me.

She pissed and came back. Outside there was the distant wash of the sea, the unkempt Atlantic. Every week swimmers drowned down there and were washed up in the villages, eyes plucked, innards mangled. She climbed over him, she wanted him inside of her, inside her intestines and bones, assimilated with the functions of her body. When he thrust she wanted him to break her somewhere, to pierce her being, for the communion to become a grieving. It was never enough.

Blake told his mother he was taking Kwesi with him to the chemist. Otherwise she would run out of the house scouring the yard for him. She was always checking for Kwesi, needing him close to her in an entrapped, panicky way. When she had him in her stomach Blake had seen Kwesi's face. She made him touch the shiny hairless skin that Henry rubbed with shea butter in the night. Blake had seen Kwesi's face looking at him, day after day, getting sadder that he had to come away. He knew Kwesi was in no rush to join the world.

She said okay with her head tossed back. Blake took money from the rolls in her purse, then put Kwesi in the old stroller that he and Amanda and Roddy had all been pushed around in. He knew the plastic tartan pattern like he knew the shape of his own fingernails, with their ridges and white spots. He put Kwesi inside and pushed over the stones outside the house where the grass would never come up. It was where Henry parked his big Land Rover. The dogs rushed around from behind the house to check on him, all sparky and keen. But they saw him and stood there. They dropped to the ground.

Opposite their house was a home for delinquent kids. Their faces were often at the window bars on the sagging building under the trees, or they rushed to the fence whenever he walked past. *Hey, obroni kid give us money, we beg! Hey obroni kid, you got Fan Ice for me?* His mother said they were unfortunate, and smiled at them at first, then her smiles finished. Now she agreed with Henry that they made a racket and were up to no good.

Today there was no one in the bright dusty yard, no one in the street. Blake pushed the stroller. The girl at the Liberty Hotel next door sat at her desk watching the television, she waved. Kwesi looked into the dark recess making out her face, he remembered her. It was where Blake and his brother and sister came to receive their father's telephone calls once a week. Their father's voice wavered and cracked and they fought over who would sit on the tall stool at the customers' desk. It made Blake's mother storm back to the house.

Kwesi pointed up to the kiosk on the corner where Dorothy sold minerals and sweets. They stopped and Blake fished out a note for two Fantas. Dorothy pulled them out of her cool-box and opened them, then she swung Kwesi up into her arms, feeding him from the glass bottle. Blake stood and watched. He wasn't thirsty, but he felt bad if he walked past. Dorothy sat there all day until she fried a pan of gingery plantain at night and gave you soft wads wrapped in newspaper to take home. The chemist was further down the road.

He pushed the stroller onto the ramp across the open gutter and levered it down the step. Inside everything was painted white and the boxes and brown bottles were pushed to the backs of the shelves. The woman wore glasses and didn't like him very much, some people just disliked you. She gave him painkillers and antibiotics, the ones he asked for. His smelly notes fluttered under the fan and the woman stared at Kwesi.

Outside grey storm clouds filled the sky over the sea at the end of the street but here the sun struck everything around them. Kwesi turned back and looked up. *Where were they going? What was going to happen now?* Blake stood in the middle of the road with his mother's boxes wrapped together in printed paper, the ends tucked in like gifts, sitting in the tartan folds of the hood. Far off, he thought he could hear the motion of the sea but he knew that it wasn't, it was the traffic flying past on Ring Road, taxis and *trotros* and beaten-up cars. He pushed the stroller on down the road, past the low buildings and houses. There were concrete frets along the gutters to stop you falling into the black water.

They reached the big road before the sea and Kwesi looked contented. They watched the clouds knock together, pushing out boulders of dirty white. All along the horizon the water was silver and flat, wearing a frightened sheen. The cars sped faster and faster.

Henry drove her to the hills that pushed the city against the coast. As they rose the change in altitude made her head feel looser, or perhaps she had just had her face in his groin so long. Now she lifted her head. The humid mortar of the city had fallen away and up here the colonial buildings stood tall, fettered with all manner of appendages, and the roads were thin, drawn over the landscape with their trails of unfit transportation. Huge old trees carried the heaviness of history as much as their scored vaulting, vegetation was stiff.

She was thirsty, the two beers at the hotel had brought it on. Now she was clammy with his liquid and everything felt flawless. She looked at him as he drove, wanting to rub herself harder into his skin once again, wanting to lick his eyelids and use her tongue to feeler his teeth. She wanted to chase him, bring him down, feed on the spurting from his neck.

'Where the fuck did you take him? Don't you know I'm in agony?' his mother shouted from the porch. His brother and sister were back now, someone's driver had brought them home. They stood staring as he pushed the gate and the dogs wagged their tails around him.

'Bring him to me, bring me Kwesi. Where the hell have you been?'

Kwesi was cheerful in her arms and she nuzzled him. Blake unfolded her change and put it back in her purse. He ripped open the boxes wrapped like gifts.

'Here is your medicine. I bought it.'

The other kids went back to the television and his mother cradled Kwesi on the couch. Their eyes met, she touched his hair, he pushed his small face to her shirt. Blake heard Agnes cooking in the kitchen.

During the night he heard her moaning. At times she panted, or she drew in a long breath and held it there, forgetting to expel. Her light switched on and he heard her fumble for the pills, drink water, push the glass over on the painted barrel next to the bed and swear. The crying started again. It was a soft rocking that wouldn't stop.

Later, she walked through the house and unlocked the front door. He was afraid then. Outside at night, it was another world. The flowers were white and drunken and the leaves ready to catch your face. There were thieves and the air was deep. He sat up in bed. He couldn't hear her. Something was going to happen. Somebody would beat her, take her away.

He ran out of the room towards the front porch. She was sitting there in the moonlight, watching him running to her, a little half-smile he had never seen before.

'Darling, what are you doing up so late?' she said. The dark was different to her, she was all grey and her mouth was big. Her shoulders were shining. 'I can't sleep. The pills aren't doing much. But you mustn't worry. Tomorrow everything will be better and I'll pop in to the doctor's after school. Do you want a hug, love?'

He came over, allowing her to hold him, which she did tightly, unpleasantly. Her skin was hot and dry next to his and she smelt of badness and pain. *Oh my baby!* He wriggled free, he pushed away from her.

'Don't push your mother,' she said with tears. 'Please don't.'

In the dark she was not his mother but a grey tricky shape using her voice. And yet she was. It was his mother.

'You hate Henry, don't you? It's okay, you can say it if you like.'

Now he was disgusted with her. He saw the gauze glowing on her hand.

'I know it's not what you'd have wanted,' she said.

There were mosquitoes all around and from the window he heard Ibrahim coughing. He hated Agnes, that's who he did hate, he knew Agnes chewed on Ibrahim in the afternoon. But with Henry it was another thing, it wouldn't let him think. Henry put his hand on his back, he hoisted him onto his shoulders. Henry's head was shaven and greasy like a nut.

'I'll come to the doctor tomorrow, if you like,' he told her.

'Would you? You're such a big boy now.'

He wished that he were smaller.

In the morning when Agnes roused them his mother didn't get up. That happened a lot when Henry was around. Henry blocked the door, wrestled with her, pushed her into the bed. He and his brother and sister would eat their cereal out the back and Ibrahim would come in with a fresh shirt. This morning he stood by her door. Then it was time to go or there'd be late notes for all of them.

Henry wanted to show her the Aburi Gardens. She had a vision of a gabled homestead and glades of mile-high trees. Mahogany, ebony, stolen woods. His family ran a small furniture business but he had taken to timber exportation. He wanted to show her the massive forests outside Kumasi where the logging went on, and the new saplings he swore they planted. He drove up the entry road with its column of royal palms. The hills fell away, people vanished. A man tugged a goat down the road.

In the car he checked his phone and switched it off. He zippered his trousers and smiled at her. A bus pulled in and churchgoers poured out onto the red terrain. The grass came up to the parking lot in a carpet spread under the trees, bird calls rang out. A young man in a white shirt came over to him and shook his hand. There was always someone he knew. He introduced her.

They walked away from the group.

She inhaled. It was gorgeous, being here. Without him she would never have seen these places, the sharp hills with their rich greenery. He pointed out trees to her. *Are they trees you'd like to chop down?* she asked cheekily. She wanted him to embrace her but in public they were chaste, it undid her at times. Inside the broken army plane, parked absurdly on the lawn, he studied her face, rubbing his fingers over her kiss. It almost hurt her.

'Let's go up to the house.'

They walked towards the homestead which had been cordoned off at the head of the rise, the wood-planked veranda serving as a bar. He ordered two more beers, though she would have preferred water. Below them she saw the grandest tree of the park. Planted hundreds of years ago, it thrust into the air with a balanced grace, broad leaves occasionally falling. There were vines threaded over the boughs and the trunk was folded with bulging growths, wooden fins slid into the ground. A pounding started somewhere in the building. Plantain and cassava and yam were being pounded to make *fufu*, a dish they often ate together. She was a little drunk but able to savour the peacefulness between through them. She didn't need to talk.

They walked in another direction where the land banked down into a grove of lesser trees. Expectant, she thought of gaudy flower beds and spiky tropical growth, the lilies she had once seen in a botanical garden, but instead the park was all the same, the grand old tree had been its highlight. She followed him where the grass was shaggier and saw the churchgoers in the distance. She heard voices, sometimes they sounded deranged.

'What is it? What are they doing?'

There was a little valley of them. Men and women in pairs, often one or the other had their arms raised, or the man held a slumped woman under the arms.

'They are speaking tongues. They come here to speak in tongues.'

She shuddered. A woman in a white dress threw herself into the grass and began beating, screaming, her mouth muffled by the earth. Her fists beat into the grass.

'It's nothing. I thought you might like to see them.'

'Not really. Please let us go back.'

He touched her inner arm and her own prayers were answered. They pulled away, back towards the car park, as the voices grew to an eerie militant level. Here he kissed her with such tenderness that her fears deserted her. She realised that this afternoon he had given her his seed.

The doctor stared into the wound. Blake's mother's eyes were horrified. The infected part of the finger had burst apart and filled with a yellow sludge. The rest had become a hard red rod. Henry's sister the nurse stood behind, her tongue clicking.

'I'm afraid we're going to have to clean this out. It's an abscess.'

'Oh God. That's going to hurt, isn't it?'

'I think it shall. But we have no chance here.'

She looked at Blake, but he was not enough. Her eyes frayed with panic. 'Can't we wait? I think Henry is coming back tonight. That way we could come in tomorrow and he could drive me home.'

Blake thought of them snaked together, the wound

kissed.

'Oh no, Mrs. Connelly. It's best we get this done now. Are you certain you want your son here?'

'Well, yes.'

'We can proceed.' The nurse prepared instruments and the doctor motioned to his mother to sit down and place her hand on the examination table. He brought over a stronger light and took her taut hand in his own.

'It is all right, Mrs. Connelly. This must be done. Please relax.'

'Isn't there a needle? A painkiller?'

'It will be faster than you think, although I will have to squeeze. Look at this strong young man you have here by your side.'

She glanced Blake's way. The doctor was calm with a green worn shirt under his white jacket. Henry's sister brought over the instruments in a pink solution and a dish of soaked cotton wool.

'Oh my God.'

Blake watched the doctor isolate the injured finger and begin to press. His mother groaned, gripped the chair, her legs twisted.

'Please Madam, you must keep still.' He plucked out an instrument and with this raised a soaked cotton swab which he put to the wound. His mother jerked backwards. The doctor frowned at the nurse.

Henry's sister came around and clamped his mother's hand to the table. Once again the doctor put the cotton swab to the wound. His mother shut her eyes and ground her jaw. Blake watched the cotton grow dirty with green and yellow, one and then another. His mother cupped her face with her other hand.

'There now, young man,' said the doctor. 'Take a look at the bone.'

His mother turned away but Blake was curious and

looked at the grey surface under the parted skin. Since their new life began Blake and Roddy and Amanda had all had boils – on their faces, on their necks – but the boil had a hard plug, you just had to wait to shift it out. A boil never went down so far and the skin travelled over the puncture fast.

The nurse wrapped the finger and the doctor washed his hands and returned to his desk, putting a new bottle of antibiotics in front of her.

'These will do the trick. That medicine from Nigeria, it is not good for the eyes. You shall come back tomorrow so Felicia can redo your dressing.'

His mother paid and walked giddily into the sun. For a minute she stood in front of the building which was an old house with the clinic installed downstairs. Across the road was a new storey block with a high radio tower. A taxi set down a woman with a sick baby wrapped in cloth. She moved fast, shoving through the pair of them.

His mother spoke to the driver and they climbed into the back. She told him the shortest way to go in case he tried to cheat them. It was a low, bumbling vehicle full of hanging trinkets.

Now that the finger was done there was nothing. She began to cry and the way the tears dripped onto her shirt Blake knew they were tears of sadness, not pain, and that her finger had been part of the wrongness they were living which could never be fixed. Soon Henry would be back, he was reminded.

The taxi drove along their road up to the gate. The delinquent children were playing in the dust and a bunch of them rushed to the fence.

Madam, obroni Madam! You give us Fan Ice? You give us cedis? We hungry, obroni boy!

His mother ignored them and pushed open the gate. The dogs rushed around the side of house barking. Agnes came out onto the porch to see.

But when his mother walked towards the house he

169

stayed there. He waited for her to go inside. He went back onto the road and the delinquent kids watched him. One shimmied over the fence.

Blake stood there waiting.

'Take me to the top,' he said, pointing to the empty building next door. The delinquent boy was taller than he was, with a small head and big ears.

Blake followed the boy to the locked gate and he showed him how to put his foot on the metal fret and use the hole for the lock to hoist his body. They jumped onto the dust below. A woman was frying fish over a charcoal cooker near the building entrance which had no door. She shouted at them. The boy jogged past her, Blake several steps behind. They went straight to the stairs in the middle of the huge room where Blake saw there were curtains strung up on wires and, in one corner, a sick man lying on a bed. He heard water being transferred, bucket to pail, and smelt more cooking.

As they ascended Blake began to see strips of the city through broken windows, and the faraway emptiness that was the sea. There were dozens of people living here, even a small chicken that went cawing away, and two mammies sitting on stools who waved at him. They charged up the stairs, swinging around the fetid landings, running all the way. At the top the tall boy flapped open a door and they walked out onto the burning bleached roof.

Then Blake was at the centre of the messy city of boxes and trees and red earth, even the thick Ring Road cutting through and the radio tower where they had just been standing. Blake ran to the edge. The delinquent boy followed him and as Blake stood there marvelling he pulled a little tin out of his shirt and levered it open with his thumbnail. He cupped his hands and sucked the air from it. Blake watched him and did the same.

Then they both leant over the edge, feeling the wind patting them and the sun curling over their heads and backs and buttocks from behind. Blake held the railing but knew he was flying. He saw their house next door. Roddy and Amanda were running down the back steps to play hide-and-seek in the plantain. Then he heard an engine he knew – it was Henry's big Land Rover coming up from Ring Road – chugging through the back streets, moving towards the house. He looked across at the delinquent boy with his small head and big ears, laughing on the wind. That was when Blake knew Henry would never heal her. That was when Blake knew he didn't care and never would.

VERONIQUE IN THE DARK

By late autumn Veronique called Heinrik. She had recommenced work and her injury was no longer the thing she had to manoeuvre around. The light had distilled, as though the winter had chosen her course and would visit their city when she pleased. After a few rough mornings when Marco had not spoken to her she thought of Heinrik and looked up his number.

Heinrik answered.

'It's Veronique. Veronique in Milan. We met in the Dolomites last summer.'

'Hello Veronique. It's a pleasure to hear you.'

'How are you? I thought I'd call to say hello.'

'Everything is proceeding quite well here.'

He sounded firm, rude even. 'Listen Veronique, there is a chance I am passing through Milan tomorrow afternoon. Perhaps I could call you back then?'

'Why, of course.'

She placed the receiver in the cradle, stepping back. There were years when she would have walked under a truck for her husband. She reminded herself that Heinrik was a wounded, flaccid man.

They met the following day outside the Moscova stop which had seemed quite central to both. Veronique saw him from afar. He was looking into a bookshop window and appeared to have grown fatter. His bottom was rounder than in the summer and, as she recalled, the thatch of burned skin branded the right side of his face. She remembered their long walk together the day Marco had scaled the summit, when her knee injury had confined her to the lower slopes and deprived her of the challenges of other years. Heinrik, a man she saw straightaway as colourless and scarred, had appeared on the deck outside the lodge, coffee in hand, and saved her from the ugly permeation of her thoughts.

Heinrik greeted her with two brief kisses on the cheek. Some of the gentleness she'd inferred was gone, replaced by a concentrate of rushed urban life. She saw he worked hard, was obstinate, often unfeeling. She remembered when he had offered her a crutch – a knotted stick another walker had lain against the rock. This was what had undone her and she saw that it was dangerous.

They strolled along, Veronique speaking lightly about her latest tests and repeated physiotherapy. Unlike on the mountain they walked side by side, with Heinrik's ruined cheek being the thing she occasionally addressed. It was a buttery, slippery surface. She wondered about the crude questions of children.

'Shall we go in here?'

'Yes, why not?'

They shuffled through chairs to a table away from the lights. Veronique removed her jacket and watched Heinrik take off his heavy, shapeless coat. She looked up, wondering how she appeared to him. They ordered drinks.

'Do you expect to ski this year?' he asked her. Certainly she had mentioned that she and Marco were vigorous skiers. Marco had gone ahead with the apartment rental as usual. He had calculated that she would be fit.

'I expect so,' she said a little sadly. For she expected nothing, now she knew too much about the clunky engineering of the knee.

Their drinks came and Heinrik prepared to make a toast, but there seemed no common cause to celebrate, even their conversation had turned halting.

'Well then. To an exceptional winter season in the mountains.'

'Yes, oh yes.'

'And a day spent rather happily this summer.'

'Yes.'

The traction in his smile told her so little about what Henrik thought of her that she ceased looking at it. She decided she was repelled, that this had been a minute disaster.

After their drinks Veronique accompanied Heinrik to the Moscova stop and he caught a train to Loreto where he had parked his car. She watched his broad hand on the black belt of the escalator as he descended.

She returned to the apartment. Her knee ached slightly from the walk home from the station. She looked at Marco's jacket on the chair back. He had been and gone, his clothes looked so arid. He had a tennis match this evening. She thought of the green balls absorbing the fuzzy night lights as they crossed to and fro, the *chock* sound of impact and the clinking wire fences surrounding the courts. She poured herself a glass of wine and sat at the kitchen table as the city grew dusky outside, traffic pelting down the main funnel out of it.

She had work to prepare for her course tomorrow but she would put it off. She looked over her early woodcuts – copied of course – and a reasonable sculpture of hers that Marco had mounted on a bevelled slice of timber. Everywhere else lay evidence of their obscure, purposeful travel. Utensils, gourds, weavings: she rarely went back to the world they had come from. She studied a space on the wall where something used to hang, and now left an absence. It was an implement she had thrown that had crashed to bits.

Today had almost destroyed her. The hours she and Heinrik had spent together on the mountain had been craven into her over these last few months. That a German tourist could appear on the deck when she had been at her most pensive and distraught, that he had invited her to try an easy walk when Marco had left her to her hobbling fate, had been overwhelming. She remembered the lake above the lodge, how she had wanted to

175

wade into the chill water – a renewal, a baptism – and he had read her thoughts. And later, handing her the crutch, nothing in her life had aided her more.

She sensed Heinrik was alone in life. But perhaps not. A divorce, a willowy student daughter. A gabled house with hedges. Or the sole survivor of a terrible motor accident. Veronique had never been so curious, so shut out. The burns scar on Heinrik's cheek, she wanted to run her hands over it.

And yet today neither of them had been close to the couple staggering down the mountain trail, all the way to the stone hut with the fire where the woman sold pads of cheese. They were not these people. Heinrik had been too busy, too large. On the mountain he had made her laugh and she had opened to him with gradual enquiry, not the scalded, whetted wife. She wanted them back, that other pair in daft clothes with sticks.

Two hours later Marco came home and showered. He came out to the kitchen in a robe, embraced her in peace. She sensed he wanted to make love. Afterwards she curled away, glad she had brought out the winter covers as the season would be quick to change.

Heinrik called her this time. She was walking home with two shopping bags, a soulless, emptying trip. Heinrik had old friends in Milan, he said, he seemed to travel around a lot.

'You're not at work, I hope? I didn't want to disturb.'

'No, today is my day off. I'm only in three days this semester.'

'I had to check in on an old friend in hospital here. I'm afraid it's not looking very good.'

'How have you been otherwise?' She wasn't in the mood for hospitals and illness. As if she needed that. Her ideas about Heinrik had shifted since their meeting.

'I'd like to come and see you, if I may.'

'Well, I'm not sure. I wasn't expecting.'

'I'm sorry, it's not a trip I had planned. My friend had a turn for the worse and I drove down last night. I have to get back for a seminar tomorrow morning.'

'I don't think I can today, I'm sorry.'

'Well, that's quite all right. Perhaps another time.'

'Goodbye Heinrik.'

'Goodbye Veronique.'

As she stood there it began to rain softly. She felt the droplets trickle through her hair, reaching her scalp. She lumbered along the footpath with her bags, wondering if Heinrik had grown even fatter, she was sure he had. Upstairs she took off her wet coat and ran a towel over her hair. The rain had lent her face a freshness, she observed. She made coffee and began to do other things.

In the spring Marco told her he was leaving her. If there were a manual for these occasions, Marco had learnt it by heart. He said their love had passed and she knew it had. He said they both needed to love other people now, meaning himself. But he said these words with grace and they were painless. The winter had shown he was a faster, more diligent creature. He would not give up his pursuits. Instead, since her injury, Veronique's incapacity had expanded. She disliked velocity, feared rupture. On the icy slopes she had felt hateful. Her shakiness made her unsteady and her expertise disappeared. Marco showered her with exasperation; she was often drunk. The arrival of spring was a solace, as was Marco's leaving her.

Towards the end of term she began looking at houses on the highland and by June had put a deposit on a small place just above a village facing a breathtaking chain of mountains. Marco helped her bring her things, carrying the boxes and suitcases of their expired life with a shamed, grave face. They made love quietly and with kindness for the last time in the new house. Veronique watched him fade down the road through the woods

177

and disappear.

She had good connections for translation work from her old university in Montpellier and had ideas for a book in her field. She wondered why she hadn't returned to her own country, and how it was that the fall from her marriage had guided her so swiftly to this place. She attributed it, some days, to the hours she had spent on the mountain with Heinrik, whom she knew she would one day call and reassess.

TAXIDERMY

Ernesto said if they ever did it again they were going to stuff the dog. It was spoken lightly and we were already half-drunk. I looked down at the lithe Weimaraner collapsed on its mat in the corner, whose grey eyes soaked up the lot of us. *No! You wouldn't dare!* Ray's eyes coasted to the office building opposite. The façade was chequered brick, the unrestored thirties style still wearing pocks from the War. A man was speaking to a woman sitting at a tilted draughtsman's desk.

Ray managed a laugh, then his voice came in a lower register, plugged in his throat. 'We took eighty sleeping pills that time, didn't we? Wasn't it eighty or so? But we woke up. The doc said it would have killed a horse.'

The pair of them laughed loudly, their Friday afternoon in-joke. The window was open and the man and woman in the office looked our way. Ray removed some chopped pineapple from the freezer and Ernesto handed him a bottle of tequila, the one with the worm inside. I watched their bodies intersecting, Ernesto's brown limbs and my brother's scrawny biceps and hairy forearms I used to tweak as a kid. He was wearing the shirt from the performance of *Priscilla* I brought,

> *A cock*
> *in a frock*
> *on a rock.*

I was passed Ray's version of a Tequila Sunrise. I wandered out to change my dress. Afterwards, the restaurant had hard lights and the huge, unwieldy bike they'd stolen for me must have belonged to a post-Aryan giantess.

I read Hemingway that week. In the morning I read in bed and listened to the aboveground trains plunge in and out of the city. I thought of all the party people rousing themselves, and all the blood-red livers squeezing out grey toxins. I thought of cell regeneration and Suicide Tuesday ahead.

Out in the dining room Ernesto was preparing Ray's breakfast. I once heard him introduce himself as *a housewife and a slut*. Ray might have hated the role-playing, but his job required a spiffy suit and a slightly moronic way of dragging back his sandy locks. Ray had an undeniable history of suits. I had seen Ray in a crisp junior tux hired from Grace Bros., performing Gershwin's *Rhapsody in Blue* on a spanking baby grand.

Ernesto had left a silk house gown on the bed which I pulled over my bra and knickers. I wondered if lovers had worn it, and rinsed themselves as I had in the bidet in their guest bathroom full of Japanese porn. Seeing it like this, it seemed all too simple. Enviable. The S-Bahn cutting through the city below with its metallic fretwork, the gasping aural whir. The onion-topped tower in Alexanderplatz pricking an Agfa-blue sky. Ernesto's intoxicating broad smile. I could hardly see the patchiness, let alone the sophisticated malady they both now shared. I saw a horizon of efficient, codified bliss.

Ernesto was wearing a pair of baggy shorts and pulling out the woven leather lead. The dog had dislodged from his place and now marked time at the front door, claws submerged in a Persian rug.

'There's coffee for you. And some fresh sunflower bread if you like. I'll be back shortly. Time for a walk,' said the remarkable man my brother called his pallbearer.

I settled down to eat, familiar with Ernesto's calls to duty. For years I had thought it was Ray who commanded this boy-grown-to-man, but it was Ernesto who provided for Ray's soul. Without him Ray was stringless. Again, I saw that Ray had out-coded me. His rules were more subtle and he moved with grace. I tore into Ernesto's heavy bread.

By the time he and the dog returned I was showered and dressed, relishing a last chapter of my book. Ernesto commented upon the weather, as he always did, with peculiar conviction. Was it merely the leap through languages? The silky dog lapped fresh water from a ceramic bowl and folded down on its mat, the morning sun highlighting the denseness of its pelt. I found myself wondering about taxidermy – what a ghastly profession – and what talents would be required to give mass to the cavities of the dead.

'You're not really going to stuff that dog?' I asked my brother's lover.

Ernesto laughed and gave the dog a command in German. The dog spread its jaws and tightened its lips in a grimace.

'This is your brother. You cannot see how the dog is laughing?'

I couldn't help recognising Ray's devilry at work and then a sadness approached me on a collision course. I drank another cup of coffee. I noticed Ernesto was holding a postcard of one of the royal Princes, no doubt sent as a joke. Then I remembered I had sent it myself, a week ago.

'Look Celeste. We received your card.' He held it up. He had neat zones of perspiration under the sleeves of his shabby tight T-shirt and I could see his calling card on show. *Housewife and slut. Handyman and Dog-walker.*

Each time I came across to Berlin Ernesto would become my cultural custodian and we always ventured out with zest. With Ernesto, I had seen Queen Nefertiti's bust and the disappointing Ishtar Gate like a blue, chipped bathroom. Despite the volume of shimmering air and an impressive sense of hallowedness, Nefertiti had failed to stir me. The bust appeared parched – even a desultory knock-off – and her spirit evasive. I tried to cross the millennia towards her brown skin and minute stature, or even understand the awkward egg-white socket. Instead I thought of Maria Callas in Pasolini's *Medea*, delivering a dry wink.

I was keen to see the Helmut Newton exhibition. Ernesto said there were other photographers, but Newton's work – so easy to like, so easy to despise – was the main event. We headed out of the station and entered a scrubbed thirties building, whose dramatic stairway was crowned by a line of Newton's high-shouldered nudes. As we rose Ernesto said he felt assaulted, then stared at each model with a fixation that made me confused. His eyes nearly grazed each woman's bullet-shaped breast.

Inside, Newton's array of works was less menacing. The Hollywood landscapes showed faceless women lounging on fissured cement, their bodies arid composites pored by the California light. There were other women stashed away in hotel rooms that were studied dioramas, waiting for lovers who might postpone their malaise. While artful, the sense of relentless construction and the mess of the set remained at hand. The photos were pinpricks, literal shutter blinks, the work of tempers and twisted cables and the hustling of the light. I became curious about the aftermath – *Now you can relax, Deborah!* – or what came before, when the model's legs were gently kinked apart, or the famous actress encouraged to roll her tongue; when a breast was made more palpable with a spray of fine mist, or a puckered nipple given time to distend.

I moved away from Ernesto. In another salon there was work by an American photographer who had grown up in a white trash country state. Everything he mapped – drug usage, fights and car wrecks – was in the process of happening. What had happened two seconds ago was still written on some guy's face at the back. Or you knew the woman in front was going to hit the wall. I felt the *crump*, I could hear the shouts and, inside of her, feel the crystalline warmth of the trip, then waking three hours later with the doorframe against a cheek. I looked back at Ernesto in the airier main salon as he viewed the works with lavish comprehension. Then back to this cluttered collection with

182

its purple blacks and fatty whites. Here the nudity was an ugly grovelling thing about to be used up. In a car banked in a field, on a slit divan with the tissue leaking.

I sat in front of the video blurb without seeing anything. I shut down.

After lunch we caught a train out of the city for the short trip to the Potsdam gardens we'd missed the year before. This time around it was sunny and I knew my skin was going to burn. As we were funnelled out into the light we passed fast food shops with huge knotted pastries, a travel agency with a poster for the Maldives. I told Ernesto I didn't feel like hiring a bicycle. We caught a bus that dropped us close to the park gates and he showed me where several of the palace buildings had been shorn to the ground in a bombing swoop at the end of the War. Shaky Prussian facades were propped against the sky.

As soon as we passed through the gates birdsong began and the deep breathing of the trees eased over us. Ernesto told me that Frederick the Great had established the massive park as his Versailles-inspired folly, away from the rigours of government and a rejected wife in Berlin. He wanted me to see Sanssouci, the King's tra-la-la rococo outhouse atop a terrace of grapevines, designed by the King himself. We set out along the boulevard flanked by splendid trees. Local families trailed along, while tourists with backpacks hiked with rather more resolution. I imagined the neighs and plopping of the horses, the way their harnesses would have been absurdly intricate. I thought back to when these trees had been spindly and the views gaping, when the air of the merchant city must have travelled over the boundary walls with its stench of birth and death. How beastly for the old monarch with his blueprints for immortality.

Slowed by the heat, we marched up the tiered path to the palace itself. It was a yellow domed single-storey building – *Old Fritz's ranch,* Ernesto joked – with moulded curlicues softening the arched windows gazing over the vista. I hadn't expected the warmonger's leisure base to be so thrifty, or poignant. From the top, we peered over the grounds with their pockets of swaying verdant growth and the sunny esplanades frilled with fountains and temples. The light nibbled statues sprinkled through the grapevines. At the end of each row a black-green yew tree was shaped into a skinny pyramid.

'Come with me, come this way.'

Ernesto led me down a shaded side path and up another hill to a sandwich bar. We ordered iced coffee and it came in tall glasses with a dollop of ice-cream. We sat down on iron chairs under a broad tree and dunked our spoons into the frothy drink. Not for the first time I wondered what Ernesto said about me to Ray at the end of our long days together, but everything about Ernesto seemed to be logged onto a single dimension of goodwill. I glanced at his heavy brows and his mystical brown eyes. Profession: *nothing*. I remembered the first time Ray brought him through my door. It was weeks after Ray's marriage had come to its close, when I still had a wrathful Michelle sobbing on the phone.

'Your skin is burning today,' he said gently.

'Yes, I believe it is,' I replied. Through an odd window Ernesto always extended his nurturing to me.

'Would you prefer to see the New Palace or the Chinese Pavilion next?'

'I really don't know. What do you think?'

'Well, the New Palace is rather ferocious. It's full-on imitation Baroque, when King Frederick remembered he had an Empire to keep in line. Whereas the Chinese Pavilion was built for his vegetable garden. It's obscene, very whimsical. It might raise a smile from you.'

I hadn't realised. Had I been wearing my severe face all day?

He found a path under the trees that led to the Chinese pavilion. Following batty European trends of the time, it was an

184

unchecked mimicry of what might be considered Oriental. Beneath the pagoda eaves there was a ring of human-sized gilded figures encircling the sage-green walls, each one carrying out a nonsensical activity and wearing a lacquered Eurasian face. Ernesto removed his espadrilles, enjoying the soft grass, and we took different paths around the building. I made out a crumpled old man holding a monkey and wearing a rice paddy hat, dunked in the King's viscous gold. But then an Indian park official ushered me off the grass and I walked back to the gravel path, awaiting Ernesto.

'You didn't much like that, did you? But what a laugh. Now I have one more small palace to show you. It is my favourite.'

He paced off and I followed him. He diverged from the path towards a grassy hill with a delicate, cylindrical building high up in the light. Already I knew my neck was burnt and tomorrow there would be a red stripe there, with welts on my forearms and calves. I watched Ernesto moving ahead. His swift brown legs were those of a hiker.

At the crown of the hill was a two-storey villa called *Belvedere*, fashioned in golden sandstone that absorbed the day's warmth. From the rear, a curved staircase wended up to the first level where a ring of panelled windows oversaw the landscape. Statues stood around the rim of the roof in the Palladian style, heightening the elegance of the exquisite structure.

Ernesto and I reached the windows of the bottom storey, where a single octagonal room had been stripped bare. Inside, upon wooden schoolroom-type stands, were photographs of the same building when it had been struck by bombs in 1945, along with several of the palaces. I wondered what meticulous mind had fitted the golden carousel together again and, after the violation and erasure of millions by another warmonger, *why*? It was a concrete cadaver staggering up from the ground.

Ray came home in the foulest mood. We were flaked out on divans in the living room, sipping Bloody Marys Ernesto had prepared, awaiting his arrival from work. He came in, threw off his jacket showing a business shirt doused in sweat, threw down his laptop bag. He looked darkly at us and went into the kitchen. I heard the dog release a strained whine and saw Ernesto scan the brass relics on a colonial sugar chest. He hauled himself up and trod out to the kitchen.

I anticipated voices or the slamming of the refrigerator door, even the smashing of a plate. I know Ray, he is hardly blessed with self-control. But I heard nothing. My leg muscles flinched. My burnt knees and shins continued to combust, as did the grilled skin on my neck and forearms. Far below, audible through the window sash Ernesto had opened an inch, an evening train scored along the tracks.

I didn't expect them to come out any time soon. The indentation of Ernesto's bum remained on Ray's white sofa. I finished my drink and left the glass on a coaster on the chest. I walked through the shuttered doors to the library where I slept, grabbed the silk house gown and went into the guest bathroom.

I ran a cool bath, throwing in some cedar powder from a Muji bottle I found in a cabinet. When the water was high enough I slid in, kinking my head on the edge so I could check out the erotic artwork they had brought back from Tokyo. The drawings were as dense as comic strips, with thick streams of calligraphy in the background. In each frame a coy female sat in a pool of gorgeous silks, as each heavy-headed lover parted his garments to reveal an engorged coffee-coloured member pushing through crimped hair. In one drawing the act of penetration generated strings of liquid.

I dozed, occasionally stirring the water so that the cedar smell was released. Otherwise I marvelled at the artist's decision to place a yellow teapot and a blue bowl of rice to one side, under a window showing shreds of snow. Or how another lover stretched his hand to give a coin to a grinning beggar, the flat woman scripted beneath him. I thought of how dirty our faces grow in climax, how quickly the skin chills.

Ernesto knocked on my bedroom door when I was browsing for a new book. I had finished *Fiesta*. I wanted something different. Ernesto came in and I was surprised when he gave me a run-down of many of the novels present. *Housewife, slut, reader of English classics?* He caught my surprise and looked hurt.

'Ray's totally off the rails this evening. I've sent him to bed. Why don't you come out with me to take the dog for a walk? Now that you've relaxed a little.'

'Sure,' I said.

When I came out the dog was at the front door, its long legs fraught with anticipation. It made no sound. How could anyone but Ray teach an animal to laugh? Ernesto opened the door and the dog hurtled to life down the stairwell. Out on the street he pulled on the lead for the first two blocks then turned around to us gratefully, rosy tongue dripping.

'I have to be careful around here,' Ernesto said. 'There's a guy in one of the bars that he doesn't like. He took a nip at him once.'

We walked under the railway bridge, then through a broad pedestrian area filled with aluminium chairs and people enjoying drinks in the evening. We headed towards the river where the last tourist boats floated by with megaphones and tanned ladies wearing hats. Stone walls kept the river in check and several beautifully restored buildings rose on the other side. Every so often the wall halted and mossy steps descended to the waves. Ernesto let the dog off in a park and it jerked about sniffing trees and grass clumps before heading to the water. We followed. We reached the river in time to see the dog lunge in, its jaws clenched like a woman trying not to wet her hair.

'What's wrong with Ray today?' I asked Ernesto.

'It's his antidepressants. They make him angry. The last type he was on made him sleep endlessly. I spent half of last year waiting for him to wake up. I've given him something to calm down. He'll be fine when we get back.'

Ray's ex-wife Michelle told me he had thrown her to the ground. Ray never knew she had wanted to press charges. I talked her out of it. Before, Michelle and I were close.

'How's his job going?'

'The job? Perhaps we could pass by his office tomorrow. Although the building doesn't treat him well in the summer. They've transferred. It's like a hothouse. Poor Ray comes home all petered out. But he's off tomorrow afternoon. I expect we'll go to the lake.'

I couldn't ask him about the other things – the illness, the stuffing of the dog, the eighty sleeping pills for Christ's sake. When we were drunk again I would do that. I had to.

The dog charged out of the water like a rubbery seal, thunking up the steps, violently shaking before us. The water, stinky as it was, was a relief.

But Ernesto was wrong about Ray that night. Ray wouldn't leave his room and the pair of us went out alone. First to a Vietnamese restaurant, then to a transsexual show called *Chantal and the House of Sighs*, in a downstairs bar near Alexanderplatz. They put stamps on the white undersides of our arms. Ernesto gave me a pill and washed his down with vodka and a can of Red Bull. I didn't see him much after that. There were booths out the back. After midnight Chantal came out in a long tartan skirt with a couple of punks on guitars. She was high or drunk and during the third song she crashed over one of the speakers and fell into the crowd.

I opened the French doors and trod onto the balcony. Ray kept his ferns out here, plus a stack of cornices and plaster acanthus leaves he collected from the antiques market. A train passed, grinding the metal with a gassy friction. Down on the footpath below, people were heads and shoulders, sometimes a swinging bag or an odd gait. The silver cobbled road followed the weave of the train track.

Ernesto and Ray came home together. They were both in shorts and sweaty-looking. They'd been to the gym. Ernesto asked if I felt okay after last night and Ray asked if I had found a new book to read. We moved into the kitchen and Ray opened the freezer, pulling out his box of frozen chopped fruit, his box of tricks. Across the courtyard, the woman worked in the office alone.

Ernesto opened a cupboard full of spirits and pushed bottles back and forth until he found a blue bottle of Bombay Sapphire Gin. He watched Ray tossing fruit into the blender then pulled down some hand-blown glasses. Ray poured in a slug of gin. I looked at the grey dog lying in the corner, gazing at his masters.

'What happened to you last night? Ernesto said. 'I came out and you weren't dancing anymore. I'm glad I gave you that set of keys.'

Though I rubbed hard with nail polish remover, the stamp from the club had sunken deep into my skin and barely faded. On the way home there had been a bunch of skinheads under the bridge. Laughter and frightening German words. I'd walked the long way home in the mauve light.

'Oh, I lost track of it all. And Chantal took a dive into the audience.'

'Yes, she's not usually so trashed.'

Ray looked at him obliquely and it was a look that I couldn't understand. Between us, some sort of misreading had become inoperable. I had lost the path to him, and Ray's interest in me had to sluice through Ernesto.

They had a small convertible Fiat parked under the railway bridge in a weedy lot with a chainwire gate. Ray was a tireless driver whose overconfidence had caused a string of crashes. I watched his satisfaction as the roof folded back in a black concertina. This was the car they'd bought from Ernesto's sister and it still had Italian plates. Ernesto opened his door and I climbed into the back seat.

But whatever Ray was on was still making a mess of his face. Today the lines were harsh and his skin had a hollow tone as though its irrigation were poor. The car swung over the cobbles making a *ruck-ruck-ruck* sound and we left the onion-topped tower of Alexanderplatz in our wake. We swooped over the bridge through Schlossplatz then over the second arm of the river. Ray changed lanes recklessly through the office blocks, skidding past the Holocaust Memorial until he rounded the tail of the Brandenburg Gates and took the road through the Tiergarten.

Here walkers trailed along twin fronts of massive linden trees, pushing prams, carrying balloons, chatting arm in arm. Inside the paths wound over and around each other and I knew there was a sun-drenched patch where Ray and Ernesto's crowd lazed on their Thai sarongs reading after work, or entertaining their adored dogs. Halfway down the stretch we swerved around Hitler's marker, a golden angel atop a tall, staunch column. She spread her arms and wings, casting her spells over his maligned descendents.

Out of town Ray drove faster as the road widened and the traffic thinned. A couple of times he crossed lanes badly, cutting off another driver who honked his horn. Ernesto didn't flinch. I almost grabbed Ray's shoulder and once a plea escaped me. *Ray! Will you watch out!* The stuffed dog scenario came to mind and I glimpsed a mass of metal and body parts on the emergency lane, with men trying to jimmy the mulch apart. It might have been Ray's stormy circumvention of what was coming to him, but I closed my eyes and counted down to the turn-off.

We parked in a cleared section above the lake. During the War plump, golden-locked children had come to frolic on the pontoons, while their fathers shed their greatcoats and stepped into bathing trunks. These big men swept into the dark water, tossing their children's torn souls into the glittering air with its faint odour of smoke. How could these giggling children ratify the grisly turn of the continent? We gathered our bags and tramped along steps cut into the land. The lake's dampness rose on the air. We reached the bathing area with its long concrete path linking stretches of pebbly beach, each one possessing a bathing facility the War had left untouched. We walked to the last section where there were several groups of couples and every so often a lone reader basking naked in the sunlight.

Ray's eyes roved over the shoreline and his shoulders began to relax. He shook his hair and beckoned me to follow him. Incorrigible Ernesto went off to the showers and I watched Ray choose a spot and throw down his towel. He pulled off his T-shirt and unbuttoned his shorts. I sat down a little way from him.

'You don't mind if I go straight in do you? I'm dying for a swim. This week has been hell at work.'

His boxers dropped to the ground and he walked calmly to the water's edge, not a twinge of self-consciousness. His buttocks clenched as the water rose over his thighs. He took a dive and began swimming.

I rolled over on my belly and felt the stones prodding my breasts and thighs. I listened to Ray's slow strokes in the water. I knew this would be my last visit here, my last visit to see Ray forever. We all knew this. I tasted the gin lining the back of my throat and wondered what it had been like to wake up after the punnet of sleeping pills. To see the glazed afternoon as it had been before. To look over and see Ernesto's sticky eyes and the vomit on the bed.

The sun bore down hard on my burnt skin. I rolled over and saw how far Ray had gone. His arm was hooked around an

191

orange buoy anchored to the bottom and he was talking to another man. I didn't realise it was Ernesto until they began to kiss. It was a long, tender kiss with Ray holding the other man's head with his free hand, massaging his scalp as though he were soothing the thoughts within. They held each other tightly, chest to chest, arms enfolded, until the kiss subsided.

I watched them as they came back. Ray was an able swimmer, though he slowed to match Ernesto's pace. When the water was thigh-high they both stood up, water running out of Ray's thick hair. They looked at each other's bodies for a moment before Ernesto removed a strand of seaweed from Ray's waist. They marched through the water towards me.

Back on the sand Ernesto threw himself on his belly in the sun and I watched the water dissolve on his brown skin. Ray pulled out a hardback copy of *Don Quixote*. The book was a favourite of his, I remembered him reading it as a child.

'I saw Kurt at the showers,' Ernesto murmured.

'Oh really? Is he back then?'

'It seems so. He said the trip went very well.'

'We ought to plan next January before it gets too late, you know. Celeste, how about joining us?'

As they chatted I began to remove my clothing. I felt embarrassed, even as Ray squinted at his book. The sun slanted directly upon us. I watched two other men tussling near the orange buoy and they seemed gingerly crafted, not unlike the words Ray had just spoken to me. They too drew together to embrace. I looked back at my brother's long pale body as I walked into the water. The stones were slippery, the waves full of reeds.

VOLTA

Soon after breakfast they were leaving for the river. The main thing, Serena felt, was to reassure Frances. Serena wasn't sure she wanted to be alone with her sister's lover, but Frances wouldn't let Blake miss a day of school. Serena sat down in the kitchen where there was nothing scandalous about the new couple. Henry showed off his Italian coffee percolator; Frances ridiculed Henry's skinny legs. Later, Frances leaned against the veranda post and waved them off, tiny tits and bold belly in a T-shirt.

'Don't have the baby today!' Serena cried to her.

The old jeep heaved past the hotel next door and over the back streets towards the frayed main road. She glanced at Henry manoeuvring the steering wheel with its column plugged into the bare floor. He slowed to let a taxi in front, windscreens loaded with jangling saints and Michael Jackson stickers, and she wondered whether his kindness ran deep or was contrived.

'How far is it to the river?' Serena said, watching the traffic. The city certainly had no hurry to it.

'You worried she might pop?' he replied, grinning. 'I'm sure she has a feel for it.'

Talking about Frances felt unacceptable, though she knew her sister wouldn't give a stuff. There hadn't been a moment since Serena's arrival that Frances' expression had been other than enraptured.

'It's not so far,' he continued. 'If there's time I could take you up to the dam. We'll see how it goes.' A fold of fabric displayed in a stall caught her eyes as she opened a new packet of cigarettes, the first in months. 'Oh Christ, a family member who shares my filthy habit. Your sister won't even let me light up in the house. You're not going to keep them all to yourself, are you?'

Serena shook up the packet, lit it for him, not liking their collusion. If she had come here thinking she could stamp some

193

sense into her older sister, this conviction had slipped away within the hour, been strangled at the house where Henry had gobbled up the children, sending them into spasms on the floor where he rocked for them, the smaller two jumping on and uncertain Blake losing his frown for long moments. They were all trying so hard in the hot little house to show their love to her, to convince her that the fluttering baby within was justified in coming to life, in becoming its treasured embodiment. The smallest – Amanda – had painted a picture of it, a twig next to her mother's unmistakable blonde hair. Henry's dark skin had been impressed upon the child (probably by an accurate Frances) and infiltrated the painting in a smudged chocolate-black. The second-born, Roddy, seemed more carefree than ever, throwing himself endlessly onto Henry's back where Serena could never recall seeing him plastered to his suffering father's. And Frances in her rarefied state seemed to her to be kinder, less testy, shorn of her chronic incapacity to see that her life was blessed. So round and thin, she oozed horniness while hardly touching him, and how they fucked in the night.

Serena watched Henry take a peaceful drag on the cigarette and exhale; the traffic inched out of the city.

Two years ago Serena's boyfriend Xavier left her for a young French photographer he met in his English class. The first time Nathalie came to the house with her big eyes and chic tousled hair, Serena knew Xavier was lost to her. Nathalie came from a feisty Parisian family and told Serena her mother was an art teacher in a French school in West Africa, in fact she lived in Accra, the same city Frances' husband had just been posted to, which Nathalie said she had visited a couple of times. Serena pulled out the atlas she had salvaged from their childhood house and ran her fingers over the brown continent, singling out the country Nathalie's feisty mother and her sister Frances now shared. She saw the terrain was fissured by a wide lake, with a river meandering to the coast. She read about the Volta River dam, built when the country was an English colony. When Xavier finally followed Nathalie back to Paris, Serena booked a ticket out to West Africa to visit her sister. She wrote him a letter and locked the empty flat.

That time, Frances was dealing with a six-month-old baby and two small kids. But they were her husband Dean's children, the husband she would soon abandon. Frances spent a lot of energy moaning about Dean's uninspired square-headedness, about Blake's burdened nature and Roddy's boundless energy, then about the power cuts and the roaring of the generator and the new clingy baby girl who was fitful, so much more than the others.

The day before she was to leave for London Serena had needed a break. She took a taxi downtown, walked through the central markets where she had her phone swiped out of her pocket and lost her way. She saw a bar with wide colonial eaves perched over a busy roundabout, found the stairway up and sat there drinking beer after putrid local beer. She absorbed every single detail she could see below, from the chickens fossicking in the gutter to the women in their haloes of kerosene light, all the way to the lighthouse swinging an indigo wash over the sky.

'*Quelle fleuve?*' the French bitch had enquired. 'What reever?'

After a brief stretch of concrete highway they came out onto a desiccated road which soon brought them to a thick barred fence that reminded her of a tiger cage at a zoo. Its gate had been dragged across and stood tilted there, flaking blue paint. An unencumbered road lay ahead. Soldiers in caps dozed under two massive trees where the chop stands were congregated. Henry's Land Rover squeezed through and accelerated.

'So what did you get up to last time when you were out

here?' Henry said. That was as close as they had come to the intimate after a safe talk about the city's traffic and the high points of its hinterlands. Serena caught the cautious tone, hoping that for Frances' abandoned husband it was an indication of respect. She knew that just before Amanda's second birthday the lovers had met in an art gallery, where timber merchant Henry Osei joked with minor diplomat's wife Mrs. Frances Connelly, apparently talking her out of buying a local artist's overpriced painting. Osei then mischievously invited Connelly out for a drink in the city's dank seductive quarters, zones Frances wouldn't have dreamed of putting under her belt. Now Serena examined Henry's incredibly long fingers, each joint stretched to an almost caricatured extent. *Gorgeous for sex,* she stopped herself thinking.

She replied, 'Last time, I wasn't in such a great way. We went to the beach a few times. I mostly stayed with Frances. She was still breast-feeding Amanda.'

He was quiet then and she wanted to say *Bastard* to him, because somebody should have and Dean wouldn't have had the guts. On the other hand, his silence was satisfying. Dean had wanted to take her to the dam last time but she'd had a massive headache for days.

'We never came this far with Frances and Dean and the kids,' she said. 'Although I knew there was a big river and a dam up here.' She wanted to make it plain to him that before this union there had been another one, the real one, the one Frances belonged to. She remembered Dean so bewildered on the phone, *She's pregnant. Serena, she's bloody pregnant. Doesn't she know she already has kids?* Meanwhile Frances gushed about those double-jointed fingers in her emails as if she'd won the lottery three times over. Never asked a thing about Xavier or the tests. Nothing.

'The river is one of my favourite places, you know,' he went on. 'I'll take you for a ride on one of the river boats and you can see the villages. The dam upstream has ruined it for the fishermen and they do a lot of farming. I'd love to move up here, grow some stuff. It'd be a great place for the kids.'

Serena frowned, considered getting out of the car at the next junction, catching a *trotro* back to town and throttling her sister's neck.

'Up here?' she cried.

'Sure, we've brought them up many times. Blake tried his hand at fishing and caught some sort of eel.' He looked across with a blameless smile. That was the problem with him, he always looked so damned blameless, and yet she knew he was tuning the moment, deflecting her scrutiny, making his overwhelming robbery seem like a small fishing tale.

'Frances couldn't live up here in a fit,' she spat.

Next he turned off the road and drove into a broad red-earthed bus station where a coach was parked near the chop stands and for a moment she thought he was calling off their excursion and sending her back to town. A stream of ladies in coloured cloth came onto the dust, all blue-and-white patterns like a selection of Delft crockery.

'I'd like to check the water,' he said. 'The gauge isn't working and I think there's a leak somewhere.' He stepped down and Serena felt her breathing quicken as she watched him call over a short man in a boiler suit smothered in grease. Henry was dressed heavily, a man who'd lived for stretches in Europe. Serena couldn't recall ever seeing him sweat. The old ladies tramped off in the brutal sunlight.

The bonnet jerked up and she was looking at grey metal. She heard hissing. She popped down and asked him, 'Is there a loo about?' He was concentrating on the man bending under the engine, she bet Henry wasn't too keen on genuflecting in the dirt. He pointed the ladies' room out to her.

She walked off to an alley-way alongside the bar, where there were benches and grubby aquariums of oily biscuits in

197

twisted plastic bundles and boiled eggs and entrapped flies, milky tea in pastel plastic cups that showed the grime and men swiping up their *fufu* in their fists. She could smell it coming at her, a cloud of hot welling pee. She approached the half-shuttered door with a lady's speckled shins underneath. She wished she could understand their tongue and walk away among them.

She and Xavier walked into a sex shop off Rue du Temple. Xavier had a Japanese friend who had designed a prize-winning toy and he wanted to show it to her. Serena had seen it online and it looked like a pebble, a gardening decoration, not something she thought she could derive pleasure from within her flesh. They quibbled at the shop. It made her think of torture devices used upon women over the ages, and how the tortured body was partitioned. She felt slighted by the idea that a beautifully conceived *objet d'art* might assist with what they currently could not overcome. The stagnancy of Xavier's job transfer to the U.K. Her iffy fertility that she knew had to be investigated. Their consequent rowing boat sex.

When Xavier inserted the thing she felt like a cold glove.

'Do you mind if I ask you for another one of those?' Henry said. The vehicle chugged out of the bus station onto the empty road running through the plains and lazy hillocks. She welcomed the cooler air and handed him another cigarette. She saw a glut of green along the far-off river bank, but there was no indication that the continent's largest dam lay miles ahead, stemming the push of the northern waters.

'I still don't think she should be having the baby here,' Serena said.

His expression didn't change, nor his hold on the wheel. 'I understand your concern. I am really with you on that.'

'She has three other children.' Serena had looked it up. So many local women died in childbirth. So many babies did not survive. 'It's a rather selfish risk to be taking.'

He smiled. 'I think that's your sister's choice, don't you? And rather late to alter now. Don't worry, we've really done our research. She'll be fine, I'm telling you.'

Yesterday she had had it out with Frances again as soon as Henry left the house. *I don't know what you are trying to prove. Please come home and have the thing,* she had cried. *You know you don't have to do this.* It was all she could think of saying with the kids looking up at her, silly Aunty Serena worried about Mummy, while Frances who had taken Amanda's sweaty head into her lap, stretched her arms in the bitten, spare house as the sea air roved about and the boys rushed outside to fight in the plantain trees at the back. *It's fine! It will be beautiful!* she had exclaimed while Serena could only wonder why on earth they had chosen each other and so fast. Frances, wilted staunch-minded skinny-arsed Frances who had shocked everyone under the sun, and Henry who must have had a vital quirk somewhere to have him marshalling another man's family and reeling out a bunch of birthing tips.

'It's fine. It will be beautiful.' Henry repeated Frances' exact words from yesterday in his BBC voice as Serena jarred. 'Hey, I think this is where we turn off.'

After a curve veering towards the direction of the river there was a hand-painted sign with a couple of Ashanti symbols cartwheeling on the side. *Queen Mother River Cruise and Chop.* Henry's vehicle rocked along the track, tree branches swishing against the windows, a pair of chickens scooting into the grass and then the first tin-roofed buildings came into view. There was a parking area marked out by white-painted rocks, and more of these lining paths to the restaurant and kitchen sheds. Empty tables and benches sat under a thatched roof set on trunks. Beyond, the grey slick of river looked frozen or lifeless.

Serena looked at Henry and unbuckled her seatbelt. He checked his phone then raised his chin, looking out. There was no one else in the parking lot, no one visible anywhere in this laden quiet.

'I sure hope the boat is here today,' he said. 'I should have checked.'

'Is this where you bring Frances and the kids?' Serena didn't realise it was going to sound so chastising. Henry tucked his phone back inside his shirt and opened the door.

'It's a simple place,' he said.

They walked up to the kitchen where they could hear music playing. A young woman dozed on the tabletop.

'Hello, sista,' Henry said with a local lilt to his voice. 'Would the river boat be going out today?'

The young woman sat up blinking. It made Serena crave to see Henry with his family. A mother and father somewhere up-country, seasoned travellers Frances had sworn. Seasoned enough to accept Frances and her kids?

'I'm having a beer. Do you feel like one?' he said to her.

'Yes, that would be great.'

The woman uncapped two bottles and called out to someone in the back room. The beer was warm. Serena followed Henry outside towards the thatched canopy where they sat down at one of the tables without speaking. Light from the slow river shifted over its inactive gauze. Serena heaved. Today she had wanted to tell him that her sister's enchantment would end and they could only be cruel to each other.

'I don't think Blake likes me very much, or ever will,' Henry said carefully. 'He's the nut to crack.'

But even this was said as though Henry were blameless, as if it were Blake's fault and he should be coerced. She saw that Henry's fingernails at the end of those long, seductive digits were almost bitten down to the quick.

'Blake's always been his mother's boy. More than Roddy and Amanda,' she replied. But this was informative, generous, and he might have thought she was coming around to his side.

She wondered if Blake would ever survive his mother's abdication and this man's cajoling.

'He's so withheld, I just want to help him, you know? There has to be a way to make him understand. Frances has been so taken up by this pregnancy, she has to rest a lot. You know, put her legs up in the afternoon.'

Serena interrupted him, 'Are you going to the birth?'

'Of course I am,' he replied, the long fingers curling and uncurling. The putter of a boat had begun to mark the air.

'Well, they're pretty gruesome.' But what could Serena really know? She'd never delivered a foetus that was more than a set of disassembled nuts and bolts.

Now there was torment in his eyes and, faintly, recognition. Surely Frances hadn't labelled her, hadn't told him this?

'I think this is our boat,' he said to her and she was spared.

They left their empty bottles and proceeded to the jetty, the alcohol and the last few moments making her feel sickly and without a scrap of firmness in her body. She paused before the two planks spanning out from the muddy shore to where the boat was stationed. It was a broad wooden pirogue with a roof at the bow and a small outboard motor, skippered by a man in a clean yellow shirt.

'Good morning Madam! Good morning Massa!' The skipper cried out with such a cheerful voice she wanted to let go of her confoundedness.

Henry gave her a hand on the planks and she felt how cool and trembling was his touch, the broad finger pads with a grease of sweat, how he gripped her until she was safely on board. She sat down in the shade, pulsing, the sun having grown since they'd left the main road. He stepped aboard and sat opposite her a few benches in front. The motor gurgled as they pulled away from shore and, gaining velocity, commenced its whiny drone.

The nearby village eased by as women scrubbed washing, babies sashed to their backs, the murky river water in ringlets around their calves. She wanted to ask him about the peace he thought they would find up here in the swampy lowlands, about Blake's stillness and how she didn't believe he had caught any sort of eel. She realised she wouldn't have minded if he touched her hand again.

Less than thirty minutes into their ride Henry's phone buzzed in his shirt pocket. It was Frances. His face immediately grew alarmed. Frances was dizzy, she'd lost a spot of blood. Serena heard him mention his sister Felicia's name, whom she recalled was a nurse. The boat turned a wide arc in the river and pushed upstream against a frittering wash. Henry called Felicia, tucked the phone away, briefed Serena, stared.

Everything Henry did when they reached the shore was disordered and tense, including the way he half-jerked Serena onto the jetty and jogged off to the car as she struggled onto the bank. He drove like a madman back into town. Serena tried reassuring him several times, but she saw the truth was that in Henry's eyes she was tainted and he was shit-scared.

Last year, her ex-boyfriend had visited this place. He sent Serena a postcard which she read on the bus on her way to work. Though he made no mention of it, she knew that he was travelling with his new lover, a thought that curdled her innards and made her cry openly, shabbily. In his tight script he told Serena that Africa was not what he'd expected. It had been bastardised by the colonials and now the Chinese were moving in; the locals dressed like Bronx hoods and listened to R&B music in bars, the national identity had been crushed and no progressive and independently-minded modernity had been allowed to flower. Serena wondered why he wasted these thoughts on her, while he made love to the young photographer and she repainted their old Battersea flat. She chucked away his postcard. Later, she wished that she hadn't. She tried to remember Nathalie's face. She could always smell it when Xavier had been with her on the way home from class. The dry sweat on his neck, it made her think of something rancid. She remembered those last few times when he had carried her to the end, how her fury surged beyond his miserable fiction.

By the time the iron gates clattered open Henry's sister Felicia was stepping off the porch and shooing the dogs and walking towards her light blue Toyota. A good deal older than Henry, another marriage or union perhaps, she was wearing a grumpy face beneath her lacquered black hair. Henry's shoulders seized.

'Hello Henry,' Felicia said. She also nodded towards Serena behind the gritty screen.

'Well? Should I take her to the hospital?'

'I think there is no need. If it comes again, take her tomorrow. She's not dilated. No contractions. I can hear the heartbeat. Call Kojo's phone if you like, I'm going to church tonight. Tell your boy to open the gate again for me.'

Henry called over Ibrahim and Felicia's boxy car revved out of the yard, fuming down the street. Serena felt that her sense of sisterhood was devalued, and that what was occurring now was part of a new sequence. She realised she and Henry had failed to craft any sort of kinship.

'Let's go and see this wounded beast,' he said to her. 'It's not like Frances to scare so easily.'

And here he was right, Serena conceded. Where others dithered or exercised good sense, Frances made explosive decisions in moments, never backtracked or sought a second voice. Rarely had she seen her sister brittle or afraid. Even at Roddy's birth, the only one Serena had attended after Dean fainted at the first, Frances had expelled with screeching conviction. That was why Serena knew it was fruitless to try to reverse her sister's craving and the way she had deviated from her life, and that she would have the baby and be fearless. But here Henry was right, this divulging of panic was uncharacteristic. Serena could only wonder if it were a filament of what he extruded from her.

The house was tidy and quiet. She expected the children were with the nanny Agnes in her room in the boys' quarters, where she huddled with them to watch T.V. Henry strode forth to their bedroom while Serena went to the kitchen for a glass of water, hearing them begin to talk. Frances sounded weak at first, sleepy, then there were yards of silence as they kissed and slithered together. Serena opened a pot on the stove and looked at cranky red *jollof* rice the kids had been served up for lunch, the gouges going all the way to the bottom where the rice had burned and stuck. She heard Henry's boots thrown onto the cement floor and the bedroom door closed quietly, with care. She stuck a spoon into the dry rice that tasted of chemical tomatoes and oil from a can.

She went outside and sat with her plate of food on the back step. Before her was a stand of plantain trees with their papery green foliage and tasselled fruit. She could see baby bananas in formation, and as she ate she studied the denuded trunks fading to yellow and pale pink. The dogs came over, hopeful and wagging, then realising there would be no scraps returned to their patch of hot cement. She looked up. An abandoned storey building stood over their bungalow and from the top she could see a boy peering out past her to the sea. She wished she could see what he saw. Then she began to hear Henry and her sister inside. Their noises were grasping and cautious and she listened to their exquisite trio, wondering if any harm could be done to the unborn child. When it was over she took up r bag and walked to the hotel next door where they had very beer, almost too cold for her liking.

ALSO FROM CATHERINE MCNAMARA

The Divorced Lady's Companion to Living in Italy

Marilyn Wade, half-Hungarian divorcée and mother of unflinching teens, moves to Milan to remap her womanhood. Rumour had it that Marilyn's old icon Jean Harper met her Milanese lover on a singles trip to Macchu Pichu and went to Italy to bear their love child. But sexy glamorous Milan is about as unfeeling as a Prada bag. The streets are full of mile-high models, immigrants and remarkable men in suits. Who will she meet as she acquires a taste for grappa-laced espresso in bars and learns Italian in a room with George Clooney?

Marilyn's entanglements involve punishing grammar lessons with a virile agronomist, stolen D&G heels and kisses with astonishing views, a kinky Hong Kong benefactor and a stirring love scene set in Venice. All this as she moves towards a dodgy Italian nirvana with lederhosen and a spread in Hello! magazine. Will Marilyn ever find herself and a way to conjugate Italian verbs?

A NON-CAUTIONARY TALE FOR MOTHERS OF TEENAGERS AND LATE BLOOMERS.

Indigo Dreams Publishing
ISBN 978-1-907401-73-2
288 pages   £7.99UK

Indigo Dreams Publishing
www.indigodreams.co.uk